JOYRIDE

C.C. STEWART

A'Lure Publishing, LLC

Copyright © 2024 by C.C. Stewart

For information contact:
alurepublishingllc@gmail.com
www.alurepublishing.net
T: 919-391-8502

ISBN:
Paperback: 979-8-9902920-1-7
Publication Date: May 9, 2024
The opinions expressed in this literature are the author's own and do not reflect the views of A'Lure Publishing, LLC

"I had a dream, and this is what I manifested."

-C.C. Stewart

INTERLUDE

As she woke up from a deep sleep, trying to raise her arm to wipe the crust from the corners of her eyes, she remained frozen as she waited for the fog to clear from her brain. Slowly realizing that she was unable to blink or move any part of her body, she began to panic. "Come on, girl, all you gotta do is blink! Blink, dammit blink". As Mya lay there with her mind all over the place and her body not listening to what her brain was telling her to do, she could not wrap her mind around what was happening.

Mya started a conversation with herself in her mind.

"OK, Mya, relax so you can figure this shit out! Ok, ok, ok, what do you have to do to calm ya mentals?

Yes, yes, that's it; chant! Nom yo ren ge ki o; Nom yo ren ge ki o; Nom yo ren ge ki o. Ok, now, let's use what senses we are able to. (Snaps fingers in her head). What can you see?

"I can see that it is dark. I see a big oak tree. I see what appears to be a roof or some shit. Ok good! Now, what can you hear?

As Mya lay there, still trying to calm her mentals, she really started to panic. Mya started to do what she thought would be crying. "I am so fucking scared and confused. I don't know what the fuck is going on. I don't know where the hell I am. Why the fuck, and what the fuck is happening to me?!!! Mya mentally screamed at the top of her lungs. "SOMEBODY HELP ME PLEEEEEAAASSSEEEE!!!" This panic attack went on for what seemed to be forever. In a state of confusion, Mya then asked herself, "How in the hell did I get here?"

CHAPTER 1

It was a brisk Monday, school morning, and chaos was the order of the day in the Shaw household. Mya was awakened by the fighting between her younger brother and sister (10-year-old, fraternal twins), the scent of the fresh air that was flowing through her half-cracked window, the smell of fresh coffee, along the strong smell of burnt pork bacon. "Damn, Gina! A Sista can't even sleep until her alarm goes off in this zoo. I hate it here", Mya snapped. Genie's deep, scary voice added to the chaos that was already going on in the home. (Genie is what they called Mya's mom's mom instead of grandma. Genie spoke with a Southern accent).

"Ya'll betta get ya asses up. Myron and Myrah, stop all that damn hootin' and hollerin' and go in that bathroom and wash ya'll assess! Mya, get ya fast ass up! Bet you won't tryna sneak ya black ass in this house at no 12:00 in the mo'nin no mo', onna school night!"

Mya slammed her body backward in her bed and pulled the covers over her head, screaming while angrily kicking her feet.

"I cannot wait until I graduate in 2 years so that I can get the hell out of here", Mya said.

As Mya slowly rolled from one side of the bed to the other, her cell phone rang.

"Who is calling this early? What? What? What?"

Mya turned her phone face up, and her mood instantly changed. Mya cleared her throat. "Ahem".

Mya then answered the phone, soft and seductively. "Hey, you."

At that very moment, Mya's twin brother, Myron, angrily banged on the door.

"Genie said get ya fast ass up. You turd burglar!"

Mya put the phone on mute and angrily screamed, "Get the hell away from my door, you lizard!"

Myron kicked the door and could be heard running down the hallway to his room. Mya turned her attention back to the call.

"I am so sorry about that. My little brother in the way, all early style. Anyway, how are you this morning?

Sneaky Link (#1) Smoove replied, "I'm doing better now that I hear your voice".

Mya's grin was so wide it could be felt through the phone. "I don't need to ask you how your morning is going,"

Sneaky Link laughed.

"What you mean by that? Mya shyly asked.

"You already know," the sneaky Link said.

"Anyway!" Mya jokingly answered. "Are you coming to pick me up from the spot before or after school?"

"I'm not sure yet, luv," the link said. "I was supposed to get an email earlier this morning, but I'm still waiting for it to come through".

"Yea ok", Mya said. Tell me anything".

The sneaky link let out a short breath and said, "There you go. You stay trynna beef with me". Mya sucked her teeth and smartly answered, "Well, you go figure out what you gotta do and holla at me., or not". Mya angrily pushed the end call button on her cell phone and tossed her phone on the bed.

Mya angrily threw the covers off of her, jumped outta bed, and headed for her closet. As Mya was opening the closet door, she heard a ding bell go off on her phone.

"This is not the mood I am trying to start my day out with. Later for all that", Mya said. Mya caught a look at her half-naked body in a mirror that was hanging on her closet door.

"Trynna act like you don't want allll of this", Mya confidently said aloud, as she slowly and sexually moved her body like a snake. Mya started feeling herself and shouted out to Alexa,

"Alexa, play my theme song!"

At that moment, Beyonce' and Nicki Minaj's song played loudly through the speakers. Mya started to do the most as she flung her closet door open and started to angrily push her clothes to the front, piece by piece.

"What outfit should I shit on em wit today?" she said.

Mya sturdied (This is a popular YouTube dance named the Sturdy) her way over to her bathroom, and right before she was about to get into the shower, Alexa let Mya know,

"Sneaky One is calling".

Mya stopped and thought about whether she should answer the call or continue with her fake attitude.

"Naw, I'ma let em feel it", Mya decided.

Mya made her way to get into the shower. The music was blastin, Mya's sister and brother were doing the most around the house and the sound of Genie's voice made Mya very angry and her body began to tense up. Mya swung open the bathroom sink doors, got down on her knees, and started to push all the stuff that was in the front of the cabinet, to the side. Mya reached her arm far beyond the toilet paper rolls and pulled a 5th of Tequila.

Mya talked to herself and tried to make herself believe, "If I just take a lil sip, I'll be alright".

Like a little kid who loves candy and just got a piece of candy, Mya twisted the cap off of the liquor while thinking whether she should take a shot from the cap or take a little to the head. Mya grabbed the neck of the bottle, put the bottle to her mouth, threw her head back, and took a big gulp. Mya's body shook as the liquor powerfully moved through her body.

"Ahhhh, that's more like it", Mya said. As she stepped into the shower, Mya paused due to a sudden dizzy feeling.

"Sheesh", Mya called out. "That's some strong shit!"

As Mya stepped into the shower, the stinging, hot water felt good as it beat against her tense body. Mya began to wash herself up and as she was washing her pussy, Mya had a sexual flashback. Mya softly rubbed her pussy with one hand and her left titty with the other. The thoughts of the sneaky 1, began to take Mya to the point of cummin'. Mya softly moaned with pleasure, "sssshhhh, oouu. Yes, keep it right there". And suddenly, right before Mya was about to cum, Genie banged on her bathroom door.

BANG BANG, BANG! "Get yo ass out of that bathroom and git ya clothes on. Ya daddy will be here to get you and the twins in 15 minutes".

Mya was embarrassed and angrily answered, "I ain't ridin' wit daddy today! The Warriors are coming to pick me up".

Genie then angrily said, "That's what's wrong wit yo fast ass now. Hangin' and ridin' around wit dem damn girls all the time. You gone find out da hard way."

"Whatever", Mya whispered to herself.

The Warriors are a group of childhood friends that Mya actually grew up with since they met in kindergarten. Mya was born in Tennessee and moved to Atlanta when she was five years old. Mya was the one who actually got all the girls to meet and start hanging out, but all the girls had something to do with the group being named The Warriors. Now let's meet the Warriors. There are 5 girls, including Mya, in their group. First, there is Skyler. Skyler is the drama queen in the group. Skyler was the one the Warriors always referred to as "does the most." She was also the one that Mya liked to refer to as "A Sista trapped in a white girl's body." Skyler was born and raised in Atlanta, GA. Secondly, there is

Rainah. She was the pothead of the group, although all the girls smoked. Rainah was diagnosed with Leukemia two years ago; however, she was the most positive of the group. Rainah also had a medical marijuana card, so there was always smoke and edibles on deck. Rainah moved to Atlanta from Detroit when she was three years old. Thirdly, there is Ktru, (which is actually said like the word true). Ktru, like Mya, always said what was on her mind; however, all the Warriors were wit the shits. The Warriors always had to remind Ktru to be on her best behavior because bitches were quick to call 12 on the Warriors. Ktru was born in Brooklyn but came to Atlanta when she was four years old. Lastly, but certainly not least, there is Asia. Asia is the biracial one of the group. She is black and Vietnamese. Asia is the calm, cool, collected, and logical one in the group. Asia is an activist. She is always involved with things that concern human rights and the rights of immigrants. Asia was born and raised in America. Her dad is a US citizen and Asia's mom has only been a citizen of the US since Asia's birth. Asia was born in North Carolina and moved to Atlanta when she was one year old.

Mya angrily got out of the shower, and as she was getting out, Alexa said, "Rainah is calling."

All of the Warriors had their license to drive. However, Mya was the only one without a car. Rainah had the SUV, which comfortably seated all 5 of the girls. Therefore, Rainah was always the one driving.

"Alexa, answer!" Mya shouted.

"Heeeyyy bitccccch!!" Rainah yelled as she came across the sound system.

"Hi, ho," Mya answered.

"Eeeee, what's wrong wit you?" Rainah teasingly asked Mya.

"Ooooh, nevamind. Lemme guess, either one of the twins or Genie, pissed in ya Cheerios".

Mya reacted with laughter. "Girl, you already know!"

Rainah then said, "Later for all that girl. And-tee-way, we are five minutes away."

Mya tried to tell Rainah that she needed at least 15 more minutes, but before Mya could get a word in, Rainah quickly said in a high-pitched voice, "Byyyeee bitch!".

Mya sucked her teeth and loudly said, "That bitch git on somebody's nerves!" Being as though Rainah was usually the one left in charge of driving the Warriors around, she had absolutely no tolerance for one of them not being outside when or before she pulled up. Rainah was known for leaving one or even all of the girls.

Mya knew that time was not on her side, so in a state of panic, Mya began running around her room. As Mya was jumping up and down, putting her jeans on, she heard a loud sound come from outside.

"BOOM! BOOM!". Mya's body hit the floor. As Mya lay on the floor at the end of her bed, she crawled under her bed like she was in the Army. Scared to death, Mya shouted out to Alexa, "Alexa stop the fuckin' music!" In the silence, Mya listened to the sounds of her brother, sister, and Genie. It was so quiet in the house; you could hear a pin drop.

Mya called to them with a shaky voice. "Twins! Genie! Are ya'll okay!!??"

Genie could be heard yelling angrily from the bottom of the stairs. "Chile the twins left wit ya daddy and ain't nuthin' wrong wit me! What the devil is wrong wit you?!"

Crawling from under the safety of her bed, Mya's clothing was messed up. Mya brushed herself off and flung open her bedroom door. Mya could not understand what was happening, so she yelled back down the stairs to Genie.

"You didn't hear those two, loud gunshots?!"

Genie sucked her teeth and answered, "Chile, that wasn't no dam gunshots. That was the muffler of a truck, backfiring as it was driving down the street. Git yo scary ass outside. Ya, fast, ass friends just pulled up".

Mya grabbed her phone and threw it in her tote bag. As Mya ran down the stairs, she realized she had forgotten her feet (sneakers). Mya quickly ran back up the stairs, grabbed her J's from behind her door, and jumped down the stairs, three stairs at a time.

Genie spoke angrily from the kitchen. "Keep on jumpin' ya ass down dem stairs. When you fall and break, ya damn neck, you gone be satisfied!"

Mya aggressively flung the front door open, slammed it shut, leaned on the outside porch railing with her right hand, and jumped over all four of the steps. With only her socks on, tote bag halfway on her wrist, and her sneakers in the opposite hand, Mya ran towards Rainah's SUV. As Mya got closer to the SUV, she could hear the Warriors trying to laugh on the low. As Mya went to grab the handle of the back door, Rainah moved the car forward and stopped. Mya almost dropped her sneakers. Mya caught up to the vehicle and tried to grab the door handle again. Rainah moved up the street a little further. At this point, Mya was becoming very angry. Mya went to go for what she had already said in her mind, was her last time reaching for the door handle before she caught another ride to school. Mya finally opened the door, hopped in the back seat quickly, and slammed the door shut.

Mya took a minute, and with the little bit of breath that she had left, she tried to yell at the Warriors, "You bitches play too much!!" The Warriors laughed. The laughter went on for about 5 minutes because each girl started cracking jokes.

"Okkkk, Sha'Carri Richardson". Asia shouted.

"Yooo! Is that rubber I smell? That bitch burnt a hole through dem socks", Ktru said as she slapped her thigh, finding something funny in what she said.

"Fuck all you hoes!" Mya answered.

"Here, hit this and calm ya body, Flo Jo!" Skyler jokingly said as she passed Mya the blunt. Mya snatched the blunt from Skyler.

As Mya was pulling the blunt, Rainah could not help but add to the clownin'. "Awwwee, is her mad? Poor lil tink tink!"

Mya took a deep, long pull of the blunt. As Mya slowly blew out the smoke, she said in a deep, smoke-filled voice, "You bitches lucky I fucks wit ya'll. That's the only reason why I haven't jumped on you bitches".

The Warriors stopped laughing and then paused. They all looked around at each other, and once again, they all broke out into laughter, including Mya this time.

"Whateva bitch!" The Warriors all said together. That was the girls' group saying.

CHAPTER 2

As the girls cruised down Mya's Street, Mya suddenly began to feel paranoid. Mya rolled her window down, stuck her face halfway out of the window, and opened her eyes widely. Hoping the fresh air would calm her anxiety, Mya noticed a black, boxed 2-door Chevy car, parked in a weird way on the corner. Ktru was sandwiched in the back, between Mya and Skyler. There was a third row of seating, but whoever sat back there, always felt like they were missing something. Mya repeatedly hit Ktru's thigh.

Tap! Tap! Tap! was the sound as Mya was hitting Ktru's thigh.

"Girl, did you see that black, boxed Chevy sitting on the corner, all sus style?!" Mya asked.

Ktru answered. "Oh, shit! Here we go again with this paranoid shit. Girrll, that is public parking. Anyone is allowed to park on these streets. Git yaself together".

Mya agreed and answered, "Yeah, you right. I'm buggin".

Mya was also the one in the group that was always overthinking every damn thing. Mya tried to distract herself and not think about the Chevy then she noticed that Rainah was listening to King Von on the car system.

Mya yelled out to Asia, who was the passenger. "Asia, sync my phone to the system so that we can get some motivating vibes goings on in this bitch!"

The Warriors all yelled out, with hands raised in the air, "Ayyyee". Requests started coming from all the girls.

Skyler yelled out. "Play some of that Cardi".

Asia answered, "hell no, don't nobody wanna hear that ho".

"Play some of that Meek" Ktru yelled.

Mya answered, mocking the sound of a buzzer when it had been hit, "Ennnnnit! None of that gets no play when I am synced to the beats".

Mya began to look through her playlist. "Ahhh, there it go", Mya said.

Suddenly the soulful sound of Jill Scott blasted through the speakers. The girls all started to snap their fingers, then they started to sing in harmony. "Ooh. oo..yea.yea". Then Ktru, the singer of the group, started to sing the rifts and runs of Jill Scott's song.

Skyler's jealousy cut Ktru off, "Bitch, you always doing the most!", said Skyler.

Ktru turned her head to the left, looked deeply into Skyler's eyes as she made fun of Sklyer, and continued to sing even louder, "Living my life like it's golden, living my life like it's golden, golden!".

Mya had the oldest soul among the 16-year-old friends. Skyler was still mad at Ktru, but she decided to now be mad at Mya for playing Jill's song.

"I don't know why she played this old hag song anyway!" Sklyer said with hate.

It was Mya's turn in the rotation to hit the blunt and in response to Skyler's high-key shady comment, Mya smoove leaned over Ktru, and slowly blew smoke in Skyler's face.

"I said what I said!" Skyler answered as she waved the cloud of smoke out of her face. Ktru was one who never let shit go so she kept being petty.

Ktru suddenly shouted out, "And the show must go on bitches!".

The air filled with laughter, weed smoke, and the sounds of Jill Scott. The girls started to all have random conversations, however Mya's thoughts went back to the boxed, black Chevy that looked sus, parked on her street corner. Just as Mya was ending her mental thoughts about the suspect car, the same boxed, black Chevy pulled alongside them and started to swerve towards the car and then back into its lane. Teasing and scaring the Warriors. Making them believe they were going to be run off of the road.

Each of the girls started to react differently to what was going on.

Mya started off by shouting, "I told you bitches that this car looked sus when I peeped it. You ho's neva wanna listen to me!" Everyone was panicking.

"Oh my god, oh my god! We are gonna die!" Skyler screamed out in a high-pitched voice.

"Shut the fuck up!", Ktru yelled as she bounced up and down in her seat.

 Asia shouted out, "Ok ya'll! All this screaming and fighting is only making shit worse. Everyone needs to calm down".

"Respectfully, but now is not the time for all that Confucius shit Asia", Rainah answered.

Then Rainah asked, "What the fuck should I do?"

In a blink of an eye, the car sped off. The boxed Chevy was fishtailing, while leaving burnt rubber marks on the road. Rainah pulled off to the side of the road and slammed on the brakes. The girls' bodies jerked and slammed back against their seats. Dust from the dirt and little stones made a cloud of smoke around the parked SUV. Mya started to choke from the cloud of dust. Mya flung open her back door, jumped out of the SUV, and started to run, moving side to side, like a drunk person. Mya took about three more steps before she dropped to her knees, leaned forward, and started throwing up.

Ktru then jumped out of the SUV and ran over to Mya to make sure she was okay. Right before Ktru made it over to Mya, out of nowhere, Ktru's body went limp, and she fell to the ground. Skyler, Rainah, and Asia were still in the SUV. All three of the girls hopped out of the SUV and made their way over to Ktru.

"Oh my God, Ktru, Ktru!" Skyler screamed as she slid on her knees and then put Ktru's head up in her lap.

"Slap her in the face! "Slap her in the face!" Rainah yelled.

"Grab my book bag off the passenger side floor"! Asia shouted to Rainah.

Rainah hauled her ass back to the SUV, grabbed the book bag, and also slid on her knees so that she was on the ground beside Skyler. Asia was shaking as she looked through the book bag, on a hunt to find her water bottle. Asia found the water and started giving Skyler orders.

Skyler, gently tilt Ktru's head back with one hand and with your free hand, put it on the back of her head.

Then Asia gave Rainah orders. "Rainah, gently open up Ktru's mouth and create a small opening that I can pour water into."

Each of the girls listened to Asia's orders. As Asia slowly poured the water into Ktru's mouth, Ktru's body jerked and she sat straight upwards while choking on the water. Asia then told Skyler to gently pat Ktru in the middle of her back. In the meantime, Mya was now in a stretched-out position on the grass, on her back. Asia walked over to Mya, laid down beside her, and asked if she was okay.

Mya softly answered and said, "I'm fine bitch."

Asia laughed, half rolled her body towards Mya, hugged Mya's waist, and placed her head on Mya's' shoulder. Out of nowhere, the rest of the girls lay around each other and placed themselves in a circle so that the tips of all of their heads were touching. The Warriors were quiet for about five minutes.

Suddenly, Sklyer yelled out, "whewww! whatta rush!"

The girls rolled around on the ground laughing. They all yelled at the top of their lungs, "Whateva Bitch!"

"Come on bitches. We have to get to school", Asia said.

The Warriors each started to get up off the ground and headed back to the SUV. The girls were brushing themselves off and fixing their hair as they hopped inside and got back into the places where they were already sitting.

"Everyone check your body and be sure that ya'll have everything," Asia ordered.

Each girl started to check their bags, areas on the floor where they were sitting, and their pockets. "Ya'll good to go?" Asia asked.

"Yes," The Warriors answered.

"Buckle up bitches. We headed straight to school, no stops!" Rainah said loudly.

There was radio silence among the girls as they made their way to school. About five minutes before they arrived, Skyler asked the Warriors, "Do you guys think that we ought to tell someone about what just jumped off?"

"Like WHO? The opps?" Ktru argued.

Skyler sucked her teeth and spoke. "Didn't nobody say all that? I just simply asked if ya'll thought we should tell somebody. I neva said who to tell, bitch!"

Asia butted in and said, "How about we just do what we gotta do in our first 3 classes? Then, during gym class, we will meet up at our spot and talk about this shit then, and we can decide our next steps?"

"Coo", Rainah said.

"Sounds good to me," Mya said.

Instead of agreeing out loud, Ktru used her hand and put a 'thumbs up.'

Skyler didn't say anything. They all looked to Skyler for her answer, and she finally answered and said, "I am not opening up my mouth because everything I say, someone has a problem with it."

Ktru yelled out, "Oh my God yo! You are so fuckin' dramatic!"

"Well, Skyler, what say you?" Asia asked.

Skyler shrugged her shoulders.

"Cool beans. Then it's settled. We'll meet up during gym class at our spot", Asia said.

The Warriors jumped out of the SUV and headed towards the school. They all walked in different directions, and neither of them said a word of goodbye to one another. Mya took her hoodie out of her tote bag and put it on as she took her air pods from her pant pocket. Mya angrily put the earbuds in her ear, pulled the hood of the hoodie over her head, and blasted her music so loud that the air pods vibrated in her ears. Walking down the halls of her high school, ignoring the people shouting and talking loudly as they gathered in the hallways, Mya was staring hard down at the floor and trying to figure out who the hell was trying to harm or possibly kill the Warriors.

CHAPTER 3

Deep in thought, Mya was interrupted by a tap on her shoulder. Mya became annoyed and took one air pod out of her ear, pulled the hood off of her head, and turned around to see who had broken her focus.

It was who Mya referred to as sneaky link (#2).

"Oh, it's you", Mya said.

"I'm sorry ma'am, but I didn't sleep wit you last night!", sneaky Link answered.

"I know. My bad", Mya whispered.

"I saved you a seat", sneaky link 2 said. They headed over to grab their seats and from where they were sitting, Mya could see outside. As Mya dropped her things onto the floor to get into her seat, she looked over to the left and noticed that the black, boxed Chevy was parked in the McDonald's across the street from the school.

Scared and afraid, Mya ran full speed, out of her classroom and headed directly towards the Warriors meeting spot. Mya burst through the doors that led to their spot, while shaking and going through her tote bag, in search of her phone. Huffing and puffing, Mya made a group FaceTime call to the Warriors. Mya knew that they were still in class, so they would not be able to talk back to her.

Mya started the call by saying loudly, "You bitches need to get down here to our spot, ASAP!" The Warriors could not only see how scared Mya was, but they were also able to hear the level of fear in her shaky voice.

The Warriors ended the call, and one by one, they all started to do what they needed to do, in order to get out of class without anyone being able to tell that there was a problem. Just so happens that the girls all asked to go to the bathroom. The 4 Warriors met up in front of the bathroom and they started speed-walking down to their spot. The Warriors quickly ran down the stairs where they met Mya standing on the end step.

Each of the girls was breathing heavily and Ktru asked, "Mya what the hell is going on?"

Mya clapped her hands in a rhythm as she shouted, "Bitch, that muthafuckin' boxed, black Chevy is parked across the street in the McDonald's parking lot!".

"Get the fuck outta here!" Rainah said.

Luckily, the place where their spot was in the school basement, had a clear view of the Mcdonalds' parking lot. The Warriors all rushed over to the window. As they all looked out the window, they spotted the black, boxed Chevy. The Warriors quickly ducked under the windowsill so that whoever was in the boxed Chevy, wouldn't notice them. As the Warriors were all crouched down on the floor, Asia started problem-solving.

"Ok, ok", Asia whispered. "Let's take some deep breaths and start to gather what we see about the Chevy".

Asia started to show the Warriors how to take deep breaths. The Warriors sucked their teeth but started to breathe deeply like Asia.

Asia once again started to give the Warriors orders. "Alright, ya'll, starting with me, we are going to slowly get up, look out the window, and call out what we see about the Chevy.

Asia slowly got up from the ground, looked out the window, and started to yell out what she saw. "I notice that all of the windows are darkly tinted. Even the windshield".

Asia squatted back down and said, "Ok, who's next?".

"I'll go", Skyler answered.

Skyler copied the moves of Asia as she got up from her squatted position on the ground. ``There are two double mufflers, and the wheels are chrome".

Before Skyler could get back into her crouched position, Mya popped up and looked out the window. Mya looked over the Chevy for one minute before she yelled out what she noticed. "There is a little dent on the front, passenger side, nearest to the front bumper".

Mya then asked the group. "Do any of ya'll remember the Chevy hitting us when it swerved in our lane?"

The Warriors looked at each other while trying to remember whether or not the Chevy had hit Rainah's SUV.

Ktru said, "**TBH**, (To be honest), everything happened so fast that I don't remember shit".

Rainah then answered while staring down at the floor, "I don't think I felt anything, but quite frankly, when the Chevy swerved towards us, my senses already said, brace yourself, ya'll about to go over that cliff".

Lastly, Asia added, "I don't think so, but I'm not 100% sure. By the way, Ktru, it's your turn to tell us what you see".

Ktru took a deep breath and quickly blew out the air as she got up from her crouched position. "It looks like the paint is chipping on the passenger side, close to the rear windshield".

As Ktru slowly slid down to her crouched position, Sklyer asked Ktru, "What happened when ya body fell to the ground after that shit popped off with the Chevy?"

"I was low-key wondering the same thing", Rainah added.

Ktru sucked her teeth and answered, "I dunno know bitch! What do I look like? A doctor?".

Skyler looked at Ktru, took a deep breath then stuck up her middle finger and said, "fuck you bitch".

Asia snapped at the Warriors, "Ok bitches, let's focus!"

Just as Asia finished talking, Mr. Junie (the school janitor), came from what seemed like thin air.

"Hey, Hey, Hey!!" Mr. Junie yelled. "What the hell ya'll doing down here?"

The Warriors were already shaken up because of the Chevy being parked across the street, so in a state of fear, The Warriors all screamed at the top of their lungs. "OH MY GOD, MR JUNIE, you scared the hell out of us!"

Mr. Junie angrily asked the Warriors, "What the hell ya'll doing down here this early? Ya'll trynna make me lose my damn job?!"

Ktru answered while still holding her heart from screaming. "We wanted to see if something was outside that looked sus this morning".

Asia then added, "Mr. Junie, could you go over to the window and tell us if you see a black, boxed Chevy parked across the street in the McDonalds lot?"

Mr. Junie sucked his teeth and headed over to look out the window. Mr. Junie looked out the window, turned his head to the right to look up the street, and then turned his head to the left and looked down the street.

Mr. Junie angrily answered, "Ain't no damn black Chevy parked nowhere out there! Ya'll been smoking that wacky weed before ya'll got to the schoolhouse?"

The Warriors all darted over to look out the window. As they looked through the window, Skyler was confused as shit, and so she asked, "What the fuck?"

Confused, the Warriors looked at each other and then at Mr. Junie. Mr. Junie said to them, "Ya'll gone and git ya'll tails from down hea and get back to class. Don't ya'll come down hea no mo when it ain't time to, or else ya'll won't be allowed to come down hea no damn mo. Ya'll unastand me".

All at once, the Warriors answered, "Yes, Mr. Junie."

As the Warriors started leaving their spot and going up the stairs, Mr. Junie said to Rainah.

"Aye, Aye, you got some of that Mary Jane for me?"

Rainah smartly answered, "I don't have it on me, Mr. Junie. You will have to wait until it's 'our time.'"

Mr. Junie was upset so he said, "Oh, I see how it is. Gone head wit ya smart ass". The Warriors laughed the rest of their way to the top of the stairs.

The Warriors all walked in different directions back towards their classes. They already knew they would meet back up at their spot during their gym class, so they didn't need to say anything else to one another. As Mya headed back to her class, she got a text from Sneaky Link (1). Mya read the text out loud but in her head.

The text said, "My bad that I couldn't meet you at our spot this morning; something came up. I know you gone be mad at me when I say this, but I ain't gone be able to meet up with you after school either."

Mya was used to feeling anger and disappointment from Sneaky Link (1), but because of what went down that morning with the Chevy, Mya now felt like the Sneaky Link might be suspicious and trying to line the Warriors up. As Mya played with the idea that sneaky link (1) may have had something to do with that Chevy shit, someone roughly grabbed Mya from behind, and they stumbled into the girl's bathroom. This person was still holding Mya from behind as they threw Mya's back up against the bathroom wall.

"What the fuck!" Mya said in a state of shock. As it became clear to Mya who this person was, Mya realized it was Juelz. Juelz was Mya's on-again, off-again boyfriend. As Mya tried to fight Julez, she opened her mouth and tried to yell at him, but Juelz passionately kissed her. At first, Mya tried to push him off of her, but then her body relaxed, and Mya started to passionately kiss Juelz back. As they were pinned together against the wall, kissing against each other, Mya pushed Juelz back in the direction of the stall for the handicapped. Still kissing, Juelz turned Mya around and backed Mya up against the sink. Juelz then placed his hands on Mya's waist, lifted her off the ground, and placed her ass on the edge of the sink. As Mya moaned in ecstasy, Juelz roughly unbuttoned her pants, pulled them off, and threw them to the other side of the bathroom stall. Julez then took Mya's thong off in the same way, stuffed the thongs in Mya's mouth, and roughly spread Mya's legs far apart. Juelz then got down on both of his knees and started sucking her pussy.

Mya's moans could still be heard, even though her thong was stuffed in her mouth. Mya started to whine her waist. With her left hand placed on the sink, holding her body up, she took her free right hand and roughly grabbed the back of Juelz's head. Mya then roughly pushed Juelz's face deeper into her pussy. Juelz started to moan while making loud, slurping noises. Mya could feel the warmth of Juelz's breath as he moaned in her pussy. This shit turned Mya way on, and Mya's pussy started leaking wet.

The vibration from Juelz's moan started to make Mya cum all in his mouth. Mya's body began to shake as she whispered to Julez, "Yes, yes! Please, don't stop. Keep it right there".

Juelz became mad excited and a huge, hard dick print could be seen through his gray sweats. As Mya started to scream out because the shit felt so fucking good, she could tell that she and Juelz were about to cum at the same time. Juelz's moans continued to send Mya. They both cried out in pure ecstasy as they both were bussin' nuts, "Oh, oh, oh, oh!!"

After they were done, Mya sat on the edge of the sink, still in a daze, while trying to get herself together. Juelz jumped up, opened the bathroom door, and got the fuck outta dodge.

"Got damn!" Mya said while shaking her head and then hopping off the edge of the sink. Mya looked around on the floor for her clothes and sneakers. She grabbed her thongs out of the sink and put them on, ran over to the corner of the bathroom stall, grabbed her pants, and quickly put them on. Finally, she put her J's back on, stood up, and checked her fit in the mirror. Mya heard the bell ring, so she knew they were about to switch to classes. Mya started to leave the bathroom, but she was stopped because she received a call from Sneaky Link (2).

"What is it?" Mya annoyingly asked.

"You wanna take a ride wit me?" the link asked.

Mya looked at her Apple watch, then took a deep breath. "Sure. Where you at?" Mya asked. "Come out the westside door, and I will be parked to your left."

Mya left the school quickly, hoping she wouldn't be caught by an opp while leaving. There was always some bullshit popping off in the hallways during class switching, so trying to leave the school during that time made it mad easy.

CHAPTER 4

Mya quickly headed down the westside exit of the school and spotted Sneaky Link (2). Mya ran over to the car, tossed her tote bag in the back, and plopped down in the front passenger seat. There was a moment of silence as they drove off the school property.

"Why you leave? You were just in the classroom before I ran out of first period". Mya asked.

"I just wanted to spend some time with you. These days, it seems like you don't have any time for me," Sneaky Link said while trying to make Mya feel bad. Mya wasn't feeling the smoke coming from Sneaky Link, so Mya came back with, "It ain't even like that. You always trynna make a bitch feel bad because I got shit to do. Besides, fuck all that; you are worried about the wrong shit right now anyway. Just know that I only got like 45 minutes to be riding around witchu. I have to meet up wit my girls during gym class."

Sneaky link looked at Mya and said, "See that's the shit right there imtalmbout".

"OMG!" Mya yelled. "See this is the shit I be talkin' bout. Those are my A ones, day ones, so why the fuck would you even be trying to put yaself in the same category as them? Shit!"

Sneaky link looked at Mya like she was crazy and loudly sucked their teeth.

"Yea. Ok". Sneaky Link said and then handed Mya the blunt that they were already smoking. Mya snatched the blunt, took a long pull and then asked, "Where the fuck is we going anyway?"

Sneaky link answered, "Don't worry about it bro. I told you we was ridin'".

Mya sucked her teeth and said, "Yea, whatever. Well, you heard what the fuck I said. You got 45 minutes".

As Mya and the Sneaky Link were driving along the city streets of Atlanta, Mya became noid and started looking through the passenger side rear view mirror. Mya's body began to tense up as she remembered how she felt when that shit popped off with that Chevy this morning. Mya closed her eyes and silently started taking small, deep breaths. Sneaky Link was unbothered, smoking and bobbing their head to the beats of the music that sounded loud as fuck now that Mya was on one. Mya slowly opened her eyes again and looked through the passenger side rearview mirror; she spotted the black, boxed Chevy fishtailing out from behind a building.

Mya started to panic. "Oh my God! Oh my God, speed up. There is a car following us", Mya screamed to Sneaky Link.

Confused as shit, sneaky link turned the volume of the music down from the steering wheel, looked over at Mya, and shouted, "What the fuck is wrong wit you yo?!"

Mya pounded on the dashboard and answered, "Go faster, go faster, there is a car right on our tail!" Sneaky Link looked out the rear-view mirror of their car, and the black Chevy could be spotted in the driver's blind spot, driving wild crazy.

"Oh shit. Who the fuck is that?" sneaky link angrily asked Mya.

"I don't fucking know! Just drive," Mya shouted.

The black Chevy, Mya, and Sneaky Link recklessly raced down the city street in a game of cat and mouse.

Sneaky Link yelled out to Mya, "Hold on tight! I'm bout to skeet off on this muthfucka".

Mya tightly grabbed the passenger side door handle with her right hand and grabbed onto the dashboard with her left hand. Sneaky link started to swerve in and out of traffic, and smoovely swerving in front of moving cars.

"Yes! Go, go, go!" Mya cheered the sneaky link on as she roughly slapped on the dashboard. Mya continued hyping sneaky link-up as she continued looking through the passenger side rearview mirror and window. Now and then, sneaky link looked out the rearview mirror, keeping tabs on the black Chevy.

"Un-huh muthafucka. You don't know I do this shit fa fun?" Sneaky link said to whoever was driving the Chevy like the other person could hear the question.

As they drove down the city street, the traffic became much heavier.

"Awe fuck," Sneaky Link yelled. "Mya, look and see if you still see that muthafucka".

Mya looked through her passenger side window and then through her rearview mirror, and there was no sign of the black Chevy.

Mya then said to Sneaky Link, "I think we lost 'em".

Sneaky link had to be sure, so they looked through their car rearview mirror and driver-side rearview mirror.

"Alright, coo'. That muthafucka fucked around and found out. I does this shit!" Sneaky Link said with their chest poked out.

There was a quick moment of silence, and Mya said, "Please, take me back to school and take the low-key way."

Sneaky Link looked at Mya with mad confusion. "You wanna tell me what the fuck that shit was about?"

Mya looked stuck as she stared out the passenger side window and softly answered, "I wish I knew." Then continued to stay quiet as she stared out the passenger side window for the rest of the ride.

Sneaky Link and Mya were about a mile away from the school, and Mya looked at her phone to see the time. Mya saw that the Warriors had started their meeting 15 minutes ago. Mya also saw that she had two missed calls from them. Before Mya got back at the Warriors' missed calls, Mya looked at Sneaky link and asked to be taken around the very back of the school.

Mya Facetimed all the Warriors.

"Hey bitch! Where the hell are you?" The Warriors shouted. Mya softly took a deep breath and answered, "I'll be there in 5. We'll talk about it then".

Skyler yelled out, "You sure you, ok?"

Mya became very annoyed and said, "I'm on my way," and hung up the group call.

Mya and Sneaky Link were slowly reaching the back of the school, and Mya asked to be let out of the car before heading to the side where the basement window was.

"Right here is cool," Mya said.

Sneaky Link sucked their teeth, looked over at Mya, and asked, "Why haven't you told them about us yet?"

Mya sat there for a second before she answered. She took a deep breath and said, "Look, now is not the time to talk about this. You focused on the wrong shit".

Sneaky angrily answered, "You know what? I'm off you!".

Mya laughed as she looked over at Sneaky Link and said, "Bro, miss me with that bullshit!"

Mya grabbed her tote bag from the back seat, reached over and roughly kissed sneaky link, opened the passenger side car door, got out, and then slammed it shut. As Sneaky link skeeted out of the parking lot, Mya turned around and stuck up her middle finger. Mya walked down the stairs that led to their spot and there she met Rainah who had opened the door.

"What's up bitch?" Rainah asked.

Mya nodded her head, pushed past Rainah, and walked in the direction where the rest of the crew was.

"Eeeee! Fuck you too bitch" Rainah said.

Mya continued walking and then she extended both of her arms behind her and stuck up both of her middle fingers. Rainah started to laugh and because Rainah's laugh was mad crazy, Mya started to laugh also. Rainah ran up from behind Mya, grabbed her by the waist, and playfully started talking to Mya like she was talking to a baby.

"Awe, you want Mommy to kiss it and make it better?"

Mya laughed while wiggling her body trying to get out of Rainah's man grip.

"Get off me bitch!" Mya and Rainah continued laughing and Rainah put her left arm through Mya's right arm, and they walked towards the other girls.

The Warriors were already in a smoke session, so Mya said to Skyler who had the blunt,

"Lemme get that bitch".

Skyler handed the blunt to Mya.

Asia was always good with reading the vibes of the group, so instead of asking Mya what happened, Asia started to put Mya on about what they were talking about before she came. Each of the Warriors was tossing out ideas about the shit that popped off before school started.

Ktru went over everything they talked about and said to Mya. "Girl, the bottom line is, none of us has a clue about what the fuck is going on."

Mya was still stuck in her thoughts because she really didn't have enough time to process what just happened with her and sneaky link (2). Mya didn't know if she wanted to tell the Warriors about what had just popped off. Mya didn't want to let the girls know because that would mean that she would have to give up the secret tapes about who sneaky link is. Not willing to risk her secret, Mya chose to say that she was with Juelz.

The Warriors were 10th graders in high school and Juelz was in the 12th grade. In the High School the Warriors went to, the Seniors went to their classes in a different part of the school. Mya thought that this would be the most believable story to tell the Warriors because they would not be running into Juelz during the school day. Asia was also very good at reading someone's energy and Mya could feel that Asia was high-key looking at her.

It was as though Asia was saying to her, "Yea right bitch. You lying".

The Warriors all started to have their own side convos and that's when Asia moved close to Mya and secretly whispered, "Mya I know you're lying. I also know that you will tell us when you are ready".

Mya just stood there and acted like she didn't hear what Asia just said.

Out of nowhere, Mr. Junie popped up from the back of the basement.

"Ya'll know you ain't got too much mo' time to be down here?" Mr. Junie said to the Warriors.

"We know that sir!" Skyler smartly answered.

Ktru was hittin the blunt and she handed the blunt to Mr. Junie.

"Here," Ktru said. "This is what you wanted all along anyway, witcho' mean ass!"

Sklyer and Rainah started to laugh, and Mr. Junie looked at them like they were crazy and smoove waved them off with his hand. The bell rang and the Warriors packed up their stuff and started walking up the stairs to make their way to lunch. As the Warriors were all walking up the stairs, Mr. Junie stopped them in their tracks.

"Hey!" He yelled out to the Warriors. Mr. Junie hit the blunt, blew out the smoke and said, "That black Chevy that ya'll was lookin' fo' earlier, was parked across the street after ya'll left from down hea".

The Warriors looked at each other and left the basement without saying a word.

CHAPTER 5

It was lunch period for the Warriors, so they made their way to the lunchroom. As the Warriors were walking down the hallway, they were talking and tryin' to put 2 and 2 together about what went down in Mya's lie about her and Juelz. Ktru started the clownin'.

"Soo, tell us Ms. Nasty. What went down between you and the booty eater?"

The Warriors laughed. Rainah jumped in and said, "Eww, did that nigga ask you to eat his ass too?"

Skyler bent over and slapped her thigh over and over, in laughter. As the Warriors turned the corner to the lunchroom, they ran into a group of girls. These girls called themselves, The Valley Chicks. They were a group of four white girls, from a white part of town, and they were in the 10th grade. The leader of the pact was named Chloe and then there was Chloe's shadow, Jessica. The other two flunkies were named Amy and Sophia. The Valley Chicks had come to the Warriors High School last year because them bitches got kicked out of their school after they were caught selling pills. You could not tell these fake bitches that they weren't 'down', as their corny ass called it. These bitches swore they were 'bout that life' and for some reason, out of all the other girl squads in the High, the valley chicks wanted smoke with the Warriors.

Chloe, who the valley chicks looked to as the 'leader of the gang', started talkin' shit.

"Well, Well, Well. If it isn't the 'Rainbow Bright Bitches". (The Valley Chicks called the Warriors this name thinkin' that they were dissin' the Warriors because they all had different skin tones). Ktru, the one who was always on the go, started talkin' shit back.

"Go ahead bitch. You already know how we give it up!" The valley chicks started makin' stupid ass sounds, that were saying to the Warriors, "what are we supposed to be scared?"

Jessica, Chloe's flunkie, replied to Ktru's comment, "Ouuuu. Watch out girls! The Warriors are going to serve us".

The Warriors looked at one another and burst out laughing.

Mya's face broke up and she looked at the Valley Chicks and said, "Serve? Who even talks like that? You sound dumb as fuck. Fuck outta hea".

The Valley Chicks felt salty, so they looked at each other, then each girl flipped their hair at the Warriors, as they walked away.

In Warrior, 'clownin' fashion, the Warriors loudly laughed at the Valley Chicks as they walked to the lunchroom.

The Warriors ended the Valley Chicks with shouting out, "Whateva bitch!" Then the Warriors all fell into the lunchroom, laughing and talking shit about what just went down.

When the Warriors were together, it was nothing for these bitches to shit on em' when they walked through. As the Warriors walked to "their table" in the lunchroom, they walked down the middle of the lunchroom as if they were on a modeling catwalk. The hatred started coming from all over the lunchroom with the whispers, laughing and nigga's whistling at them and shit. This kept happening until the Warriors sat down at their table. They all sat down, pulled out their lunches, and started talking about their plans after school. None of the Warriors had jobs because their families wanted them to focus on school and graduate, so they did not have to work. All of the Warriors were A and B students, and Asia was the only one who was in an after-school program.

Asia started out, "Well, I have my Advocates Group, for 2 hours today after school".

Rainah then said, "I don't have shit to do". Ktru, Sklyer, and Mya all said what Rainah said.

Mya said, "It's Friday bitches. Do ya'll want to meet up at my house 'round 5 tonight?"

The Warriors all looked around at each other and agreed.

"I'm down", said Ktru.

"Yea, me two", said Rainah.

Skyler then said, "Yea me three. Cause we need to figure this shit out!".

Mya got a 911 text from sneaky link (2).

The text read 'meet me outside ASAP. I have some info on that car'.

Mya quickly popped up from their table and started packing up all her shit. The Warriors looked at Mya like she had lost her mind.

Asia asked Mya. "Are you ok girl? Where the hell are you going?"

Mya grabbed her phone off of the lunch table and as she was running off, she said to the Warriors, "I swear I will let ya'll know what's goings on, tonight!"

Mya ran out of the lunchroom and headed out the school. As she walked over to the car, sneaky link let the passenger side window down and yelled, "Hurry up! Come on before we git caught".

Mya snatched open the door, hopped in the passenger side, and sneaky link pulled off before Mya could even close the door.

Mya and sneaky link drove about 10 minutes away from the High (that was the actual name of the High School they went to) and parked in a hotel parking lot. Sneaky link turned off the car and turned their body so that they were looking at Mya.

Sneaky link started out by asking, "Are you ok?"

"Yes, I'm fine, thank you". Mya answered, "So, tell me what you know".

Sneaky link took a long breath before answering. "Well, for starters, that Chevy is stolen. Word around the hood is that this dude named Pooh got carjacked a few days ago".

Mya then asked, "So are you telling me that this dude Pooh, is the owner of the black Chevy?"

"Exactly", sneaky link answered.

Mya then asked, "So, do you know anything about this Pooh nigga?"

Sneaky link turned back around in their seat and stared out the window, not making eye contact with Mya. Mya got mad and annoyed.

"Well?!" Mya shouted.

Sneaky link, softly whispered, "This is the nigga that the streets is saying, had something to do with your older, twin brother getting killed".

Mya swung her body around in the passenger seat, slumped down in her seat, and started ballin'.

Mya had three older brothers and a sister, who were 18-year-old triplets. 1 girl and 2 boys. Mya's older sister Mychelle was away in college. Mya's 2 brothers were identical twins, and their names are Mycheal and Mykel. Mykel was killed two years ago because he was at the wrong place at the wrong time. The murder is still unsolved and there is still an open case. No one has seen or heard from Mycheal since Mykel's murder.

Sneaky link reached over to comfort Mya by putting their arms around Mya's upper body. Mya began to cry more as she sank deeper into sneaky link's arms. The two of them sat in silence for a minute. Mya's sadness quickly turned to anger.

Mya snatched away from the sneaky link, looked them dead in the eye and angrily said, "You find out EVERYTHING you can about this muthafucka".

Sneaky link looked at Mya with that same energy and said, "You already. I gotchu babe!"

Mya was not feelin' the thought of going back to school, so she told sneaky link to take her home. The whole ride to Mya's crib was rode in silence.

On the ride to Mya's house, Mya started overthinking, as always. Mya started talking to herself in her head. *'Who the fuck is this nigga? And why is this my first time ever hearing that he had something to do with my brother's murder? If this nigga had something to do with Mykel, does that mean he is trying to line me up to be next? Who the fuck would be trying to kill me and my squad? Why? Damn, this nigga knows where my family lays their head. What if he tries to come in and kill us in our sleep? I gotta tell Genie to get that Ring Alarm system ASAP. Whoever is out to get me, are they going to try to go at the Warriors too? Do they know where Mychelle goes to college? Will they try to go get her at college?*

Mya's brain convo was cut off by the sound of sneaky link saying, "Aye yo. We here".

Mya quickly shook her head to refocus then answered, "Oh, ok". Mya grabbed all her things from the back seat and before she got out of the car, she turned her body to face sneaky link.

Mya said to sneaky link, "Look at me".

Sneaky link turned their body to face Mya.

Mya grabbed their face, looked them deep in the eyes and said, "Promise me, that you gonna do everything you can to get to the bottom of this."

Sneaky link gave Mya the same look and said, "I got you boo. Always and forever!"

The two of them went hard, like they were about to fuck, as they kissed each other.

"Thank you", Mya softly whispered, as she pressed her forehead against sneaky link's forehead. Mya turned around to get out of the car and as she was getting out, sneaky link reached over and smacked Mya on the ass. Mya turned around and sexually stuck out her tongue and then walked around the corner towards her house.

CHAPTER 6

Mya walked into the house, already knowing that Genie was not there because it was Friday and that was her bingo night. Genie would be at bingo until 11 pm that night. The twins were also not there because they go over to their dad's house every weekend. Mya kicked off her sneakers at the door, threw her keys on the coffee table by the door, and dropped her tote bag on the floor. Mya made her way upstairs to her room, so that she could get in the shower and get ready for the Warriors to come over that night. As Mya was walking up the stairs, her phone rang, and she was getting a call from her older sister Mychelle. Mya looked at the phone and sucked her teeth. She sucked her teeth because every time Mya and Mychelle talked, Mychelle was always asking Mya what she was doing with her life, like Mya was some type of loser. Mychelle was always cussin' Mya out and telling Mya what she should and should not be doing.

Mya answered the phone only because she had not heard from her sister in a long time. Plus, with all of the shit that popped off that day, Mya needed to talk with somebody that she could trust, other than the Warriors. Mya took a deep breath and answered the phone. "Hey sissy!" Mya yelled.

"What's up beautiful?" Mychelle said to Mya.

Mya smiled as she really did miss and love her sister, but Mychelle be doing the most sometimes. Mya continued to walk up the stairs as she talked to Mychelle.

"Nothing much these days", Mya lied. Mya wanted to tell Mychelle, but in the back of her mind, she knew that she could not tell Mychelle about what popped off because she would worry. It should be noted that Mya does not cuss when she speaks to Mychelle because Mychelle would always say,

"Is that all you know how to do? Use curse words? You need to step up your vocabulary game," blah, blah, blah.

Mya said, "I just walked in the house from a long day of school."

"Are Genie and the twins there? Mychelle asked.

"No, Mya answered. The twins are at daddy's and Genie is at bingo and she won't be back until 11 tonight."

"Oh, okay." Mychelle answered.

Mya started walking into her room while she was still on the phone with Mychelle. As Mya plopped down on her bed, she heard a loud bang on her window. Mya quickly jumped up, scared to death, and she looked out her window. Juelz was outside her window, banging on her window and telling Mya to let him in.

"Sissy, Imma call you right back. I gotta take this call real quick", Mya said to Mychelle. "Ok, beautiful. Make sure you call me right back. I need to talk to you about something," Mychelle said.

"I got you," Mya said as she tried to quickly get Mychelle off the phone without Mychelle knowing that something was going on.

"Okay, bye. Love you," Mychelle said.

Mya kissed the phone, said, "Love you more," and then hung up. Mya darted over to her window, opened it, and said to Juelz,

"what the fuck is wrong wit you nigga? You trynna have these white people call dem boys on ya stupid ass. You look like you trynna pull a B and E my nigga."

Juelz jumped from the outside into Mya's room.

Mya then looked out of her window and said to Juelz, "Damn nigga is you spiderman or sum shit? How the hell did you get up here?"

Juelz just looked at Mya, laughed, and then sucked his teeth.

"What's up big head?" Juelz said to Mya. "Ain't shit. What the fuck is you doing here nigga, is the fuckin' question?" Mya snapped. Juelz sat down on the edge of Mya's bed. Juelz licked his lips, looked Mya in the eyes, and said, "I came here to finish what we started in the bathroom earlier". Mya plopped down on the bed beside Juelz, slammed her body back against her bed, took a deep breath, and said, "Really Juelz?" Juelz laid down beside Mya and started kissing her. Mya was pulling away from Juelz as he was kissing all over her. "Juelz please stop. I really am not in the mood for this shit right now. I had a long, crazy ass day and a bitch just wants to get in the shower and chill for a second. Get my mind right and shit". Mya said.

Juelz looked over at Mya and said, "For real nigga? If you felt like that, then why the fuck you let me in here yo?"

Mya quickly sat up, looked at Juelz and yelled, "Be for real nigga! The only reason why I let ya dumb ass in here is because I didn't want nobody calling the cops on, ya stupid looking ass. Outside my fuckin window lookin' in like a fuckin' nut!"

"Whateva nigga", Juelz said to Mya.

Juelz plopped his body down on the bed and Mya got up, walked over to the other side of her bed, and lay down.

Juelz got up, looked at Mya like she was crazy, and then asked her, "you want me to leave yo?"

Mya sucked her teeth and answered, "Juelz, leave, stay, do what you feel".

Low key, Mya really didn't want Juelz to leave, but she couldn't let him know that. Juelz looked at Mya and as he was leaving, Mya said, "Juelz, please lose my number".

Juelz turned around and said, "You corny ass fuck yo. All you had to do is tell me that you didn't want me to leave. You always doin the most".

Juelz took off his sneakers and dove onto the bed beside Mya and started tickling her.

"Ion knows why you always trynna act so tough wit me and shit", Juelz said to Mya.

Juelz kissed Mya on the lips and softly whispered to Mya, "You know you love me".

Mya looked at Juelz and then they busted out laughing.

"Whateva nigga," Mya said. "On some real shit though, I just need to be spooned until I fall asleep. I had a long fucking day, and a bitch just need to be held".

Juelz softly kissed Mya all over her face and then took his hand and caressed her face and said, "You know I got you stink".

Mya and Juelz lay in her bed. Juelz got behind Mya, tightly wrapped his arms around her body and Mya slowly drifted off to sleep.

While she was sleeping, Mya had a bad dream. The dream started with Mya and the Warriors trapped inside of this big, dark warehouse. The Warriors walked around this warehouse and none of them had a clue, where they were and what the fuck was going on. In the dream, Mya and the Warriors found some steps and for some reason, the Warriors decided to walk up the dark stairs. As they were walking up the stairs, something or someone grabbed Mya's ankles. Mya started screaming and kicking her legs. The Warriors started yelling and out of nowhere, gunshots started to ring out. The Warriors could see the sparks from the gunshots. The Warriors started haulin' ass up the stairs. They got to the top of the stairs and a group of people wearing masks shined a bright ass light on their faces. The Warriors were screaming and started fighting for their lives. Out of nowhere, one of the masked men, snatched Mya by her shirt, and dragged her over towards what looked like a balcony. Then two men picked Mya up; one grabbed Mya's feet and the other man grabbed Mya's upper body as the men swung Mya back and forth, getting ready to throw her over the balcony, in real life, Mya jumped up out of the nightmare and screamed so loud, that she scared the shit out of Juelz.

Juelz got mad and yelled, "Yo, what the fuck is you going through?"

Mya's heart was beating fast, and her face and neck were dripping with sweat.

Mya sat up in her bed, holding her heart and she said to Juelz, "I had a fucked-up dream, my bad".

Mya was about to tell Juelz what had been going on with the black Chevy, but right before Mya could start telling Juelz about what jumped off, Mya heard Genie calling her name from downstairs.

"Oh, shit!" Mya said. You have to go yo! Mya said to Juelz.

As Juelz and Mya walked to the window so that he could leave out the window, Mya heard Genie turning her bedroom doorknob. Juelz slid under Mya's bed like he was sliding into home base in baseball. Mya jumped on top of her bed as Genie opened the door.

"What the hell are you doing?" Genie asked Mya.

"I just woke up". Mya answered.

"I know I ain't crazy. Why the hell was you up here screamin' and hollerin' and carryin' on?" Genie asked Mya.

Mya sucked her teeth and answered, "I was having a bad dream, Genie."

Genie looked at Mya and shook her head and said to Mya, "Don't be sucking ya damn teeth at me chile. That's what happens when ya fast ass stay out there, rippin' and runnin' and gettin' into all types of shit in them damn streets!"

Mya looked at Genie like she was some type of wizard or something.

Mya said to herself, "How the fuck does she know about what's been going on wit me?"

CHAPTER 7

Mya took a long breath and answered, "Genie ain't nobody doing nuthin' out there in dem streets. I just had a bad dream, period".

Genie looked at Mya, looked around the room, and as she was closing the door Genie said to Mya, "What's done in the dark, comes to the light Mya. Well, I'm on my way back to bingo. I just came back home because I forgot my lucky coffee cup. I'll be back a little later than 11 tonight".

Mya looked at Genie, raised her eyebrow, and said to Genie, "Where you are going?"

Genie looked at Mya, rolled her eyes, and then answered, "I gotta go see a man about a horse".

Mya and Genie looked at each other and they started laughing.

Genie shut the door and headed downstairs. Juelz was about to come from under the bed, but Mya stopped him.

"Shhh, wait til I hear my Genie shut the door". Mya and Juelz waited in silence for the sound of the front door closing. It seemed like they were waiting forever. Finally, they heard Genie slam the front door. Juelz got up from under the bed and sat on the edge of Mya's bed.

Juelz looked at Mya and said, "so, you gonna tell me what happened or what?"

Mya thought about it for a minute about having to rat herself out if she told Juelz what happened. Mya looked at the time and as she was trying to think of a lie, she was getting a FaceTime call from Asia.

Mya whispered under her breath, "Thank God!"

Juelz looked at Mya and knew who was calling and sucked his teeth. Before Mya could say anything else, Juelz said, "Don't even bother yo". I'll see myself out the front door".

As Juelz was leaving, Mya blew him a kiss and then answered the call. "Hey bitch! Mya said to Asia. What's the deal?"

Asia did not answer, and Mya could see that Asia looked scared as shit.

"Bitchhhh! What the fuck is going on Asia?" Mya yelled.

Mya was yelling at the top of her lungs because Asia continued to sit on the FaceTime call, looking lifeless. Mya was pleading for Asia to give her some type of clue as to what the fuck was going on.

Mya started to panic, and she was not sure what to do, so Mya quickly ran to open her bedroom door and she yelled out to see if Juelz was still in her house.

Mya opened the door and screamed, "Juelllllllzzzzz. YOU STILL HERE???". Juelz was, in fact, still in Mya's house. Juelz had only made it to the bottom step.

Juelz was not sure what the fuck was going on, so he ran back up the stairs, jumping up two stairs at a time, and headed straight for Mya's room. Huffing and puffing and out of breath, with what little air he did have left, Juelz asked Mya, "What the fuck is up, Mya?!" For some reason, Mya was unable to get the words out to tell Juelz what was going on, so instead, she just kept pointing at the phone as she was showing Juelz what Asia looked like. Juelz looked at the FaceTime and could see that Asia was shaking, with tears running down her face.

Juelz angrily asked Asia, "What the fuck is going on Asia? Please don't tell me that this is one y'alls little fuckin' pranks?"

Asia was so scared that she could not even speak, so instead, all Asia did was shake her head no, really fast.

Juelz was now concerned. Juelz was from the streets, so he was quick on his toes with this type of shit. Without question, Juelz started telling Asia what to do.

"Shake your head yes, if you are in trouble?" Juelz ordered. Asia shook her head yes.

"Ok, Ok, Ok. Blink your eyes to let me know the number of people, other than you, that are there with you", he said.

Asia started blinking really fast. Asia was blinking so fast, that it was damn near impossible to tell how many people were there. Juelz became a little upset, so he paused and took a deep breath.

Juelz breathed out and said to Asia, "Shake your head yes, if the person has a gun".

Juelz and Mya waited in suspense for Asia's answer. Asia did not shake her head either yes or no, instead, Asia put up a sign that read, "GET TO THE WAREHOUSE OVER ON WINDING WAY, NOW!".

As soon as Mya and Juelz finished reading the sign, the call was disconnected.

Juelz and Mya looked at each other and Mya asked Juelz, "Did you drive here? We have to get over there ASAP!"

Juelz knew that Mya would feel some type of way if he told her that he was dropped off, so instead, Juelz said to Mya, "Don't you know where the keys to your Genie's old bucket are?"

Mya quickly headed towards Genie's room to get the keys because she knew exactly where Genie had hidden them. Mya ran into Genie's room, making sure to be careful to put everything back the way it was. Genie somehow, always knew when someone had been creeping around in her bedroom. Mya ran over to Genie's closet, pulled out her Pop-Pop's old blue suede shoes, went into the left shoe, and got the keys.

"Got em'!", Mya said with excitement.

"Let's go, let's go! "Juelz ordered.

Mya and Juelz ran down the stairs and headed towards the kitchen, to get to the garage. As they were running through the kitchen, Juelz grabbed 2 of the biggest butcher knives that Genie had on the counter. He put one in his front waist and then handed the other one to Mya and told her to hold onto it until they got out of the car. Without any question, Mya safely grabbed the knife from Juelz, by the handle, and jetted through the kitchen door that led to the garage.

The car doors were already opened because Genie's bucket was an old, beat-up 2 door escort and nobody wanted that car, but her. Genie kept it all these years because it was the car that she and Pop-Pop first made out in, 50 years ago.

Mya and Juelz quickly hopped in the bucket and Mya handed the knife to Juelz. Mya paused to think about something for a minute.

Mya then said to Juelz, "why did you even hand me the knife if you knew that I was just going to hand you the knife as soon as we got in the car?"

Juelz looked at Mya like she had 8 heads and said, "Are you being fucking serious right now? Your friend's fucking life is in danger and you wanna argue about when I handed you a fucking knife? Focus on getting this muthafucker started yo!"

Mya knew she was tripping and could not actually believe that she had just said that at a time like this, so she did not even bother to respond. Mya pumped the gas pedal about 5 times and then she turned the car key to start the car. Mya did this movement about 3 times before the car finally started. The bucket slowly started up and the garage started to quickly fill up with smoke and fumes from the exhaust pipe.

Juelz jumped out of the car and manually picked up the garage door because, for some strange reason, the automatic sensor had been disabled. As Mya backed the car out of the garage, Fast and Furious style, Juelz slammed the garage door shut and then quickly hopped back into the moving car. Mya fishtailed out of the driveway and quickly headed down the Ave towards Winding Way. As they were driving down the street, Mya was driving so fast that she almost side-swiped a few parked cars.

"Yo! Do you need me to drive?" Juelz asked.

"I got this", she said.

Juelz looked at Mya and then said, "Yeah, well you might wanna tighten up before you get us pulled the fuck over and then we'll have a whole nutha' situation".

Mya looked at Juelz and could not believe that she was about to say this to him, but Mya said, "Yea, you right", and she slowed down. Juelz started to come up with a get-in and get-out plan. "Alright, yo. We need to talk about how we gonna go about this shit once we get there."

"First, we gone park about ½ block away from the warehouse. You gonna leave the keys in the car but put them right under the driver's seat. You gone take the knife and put it in the front of your pants, waistline. You gone put the handle inside your pants and pull your shirt so the blade is not showing. We gotta stay to the left of the Warehouse, matta fact, just follow everything I do. Keep in mind there is only one way in that jawn, but there are a lot of places to get out. We gone silently go through the door and remember to stay low the entire time. Any questions?"

Mya looked at Juelz, grabbed his face, and gave him a passionate kiss, and then she said to him, "I love you."

Juelz looked back at Mya and said, "Always and forever."

Mya and Juelz were cruising along Aura Avenue, and Mya said to Juelz, "We are almost there. Which alley should I go down?"

Juelz answered, "Go down Shape Street and then park behind the dumpster."

Mya slowly drove down Shape Street and as Mya was going down the alley, Juelz was scanning the area in search of anything that looked suspect.

"Alright, Alright. Park right here," Juelz said.

Mya hit her headlights and slowly pulled behind the dumpster. As Mya and Juelz drove down Shape Street, she began to feel sick. Mya ran to the side of the dumpster, leaned forward, and started throwing up.

"You alright?" Juelz asked her.

Mya looked at Juelz and said, "Yea, I'll be okay. I think it's just my nerves."

Juelz and Mya headed to the front of the building, towards the entrance. As Juelz and Mya were getting low, heading towards the warehouse, Juelz put his arm out behind him, and said to Mya, "Give me your hand."

Mya was going through so many emotions at one time. She felt scared and afraid, and most of all, she felt safe, secure, and protected because of Juelz. Juelz slowly opened the front door to the warehouse, and Mya followed him. It was pitch black inside the warehouse. Out of nowhere, Mya got a flashback about the bad dream that she just had, right before she got that FaceTime call from Asia. Mya's hands became sweaty, and Juelz could feel the moisture in Mya's grip.

"Relax, I got you," he whispered to her.

Mya took about 3 deep breaths, and before she could blow the air out from her last deep breath, the bright warehouse lights quickly lit up the place, and a large group of people jumped out and yelled, "SURPRISE!!!!!"

Juelz and Mya stood straight up from their squatted positions and Juelz was smiling. Mya playfully started hitting on Juelz while saying, "OMG, you play too fucking much."

Mya stood in place for a couple of minutes with her hands over her mouth in disbelief and also giving herself time to allow her emotions to settle. Mya slowly started to spin around to admire all the decorations, bright lights,11111, and all of the people at the celebration. Rainah came from outta nowhere and yelled out to Mya,

"I know you didn't think we forgot about your birthday bitch!"

All of the Warriors rushed over to Mya and smothered her with hugs and kisses. As all 5 of the girls hugged and rocked back and forth, Mya started to question the Warriors.

"How did you whores set all this up without me knowing?" Mya asked.

Skyler teasingly stuck out her tongue and answered, "Bitch, you know how we do."

The Warriors laughed and then Asia said to Mya, "Come on bitch, let's go around and do a meet and greet".

Asia and Mya interlocked arms and started to work the room. Mya and Asia walked toward a large group of boys that were in the corner of the warehouse smoking weed and talking shit. Asia walked over to a boy named Yao, put her arms around his neck, and kissed him. Yao has been Asia's on again and off again, boo thing, since the 6th grade.

Mya looked at Asia, as Juelz came up from behind Mya and hugged her around the waist, and said to Asia, "Bitch, you deserve a mutherfucking Academy Award for that damn performance you put on!"

Asia laughed as Yao chimed in and said, "Yea you like that huh? I was her coach."

Yao, Asia, Juelz, and Mya started laughing. Mya and Asia started to talk about what they had planned for the party and Juelz and Yao were talking, but Mya and Asia could not hear them. In the meantime, the rest of the Warriors made their way over to where Mya and Asia were standing. Following up behind the Warriors were a group of 3 young men. Their names were Steph, Rock, and Jihad. This group of 3 young men were the boyfriends of Rainah, Skyler, and in the first grade. Ktru, Yao, Juelz, Steph, Rock, and Jihad, were all in the 12th grade and they have been boys since their group went by the name, "The Brothers."

Ktru looked around at the Warriors and said, "Alright bitches. Later for all this standing around and chit-chattin' shit. It's Friday night, and it's our girl's birthday, so let's git litty!"

The Warriors screamed and headed to the dance floor.

As Mya headed to the dance floor she asked Juelz, "Where's the drinks at?"

Juelz looked at Mya and answered while pulling out a bottle of Hennessy, "You already know I got you stink."

Mya grabbed the bottle out of Juelz's hand and started twerking her way over to the center of the dance floor. Mya popped open the bottle of Hennessy and started to take it to the head and as Mya twerked on the dance floor, the guests started to hype her up.

"Aye, Aye, Aye!" The onlookers screamed.

Rainah then said to Mya, " Give me your phone bitch so I can put this up on the Gram". Rainah started recording on Live and said, "Yeah bitches. We outchea! It's my bitches birthday!"

As Mya was making her way down to the floor with her Megan knees, the Warriors' favorite party song came on. It was a song by Sexxy Red.

All the ladies at the party started to sing along with the song, "If you see me and you tryna see what's up, (skee-yee)". The song got Rainah so hyped that when she heard the beat drop, she immediately ended the Live.

CHAPTER 8

Mya was in the middle of the dance floor, sipping on her Hennessy, smoking weed, and enjoying herself. Mya looked over to the left side of the warehouse and all of a sudden, the black boxed Chevy came crashing through the Warehouse window. Everybody in the warehouse started scattering in different directions. The Warriors were all screaming as they headed up the nearest flight of stairs. Suddenly, a loud sound rang through the Warehouse. Mya knew for sure that this was a gunshot. The Warriors headed to duck cover, behind what looked like a large broiler. The Warriors were behind the broiler, and they all fell down and sat as close as they could to one another. They were breathing heavily and out of thin air, the Brothers joined them behind the broiler.

Mya started crying and Juelz immediately made his way over to comfort her.

Juelz wrapped his arms around Mya, and she started screaming out, "Why the fuck is this shit happening to me!"

Everyone that was camped out behind the broiler, was speechless.

Juelz kissed Mya on the forehead and answered, "I have no fuckin' idea what the fuck is goings on, but trust, that won't be fa long!"

The Warriors and the Brothers, all sat quietly behind the broiler for about five minutes before Jihad said, "Alright ya'll, we've been sittin' up here for about ten minutes. We got to go back downstairs and get some shit straight before we bounce up outta here because you know 12 is going to be here soon".

Everyone looked around, agreed and they all started to get up to slowly head towards the stairs. The Brothers ordered the Warriors to remain behind them and be quiet. The Brothers slowly headed down the stairs while looking around to make sure that the coast was clear.

Once the Brothers saw that it was safe for the Warriors to come down, Jihad yelled out "Alright ya'll. It's all good".

The Warriors walked down the stairs and started looking around.

"Some fucking birthday party this was", Mya said.

Rock looked around and said to everyone, "Alright yo. We all gotta walk around this jawn and wipe down anything that we touched as well as grab anything that has our governments on it".

They all noticed that the black-boxed Chevy was no longer in the Warehouse, but no one seemed to be too concerned about that at the time. Everyone started scrambling around the Warehouse wiping down everything that they could remember touching and grabbing bottles.

The Warriors said, "we all good".

The Brothers all said, "Same".

Mya looked at everyone and said, "We can all link up at my house".

They all answered, "coo".

The gang walked out the front door and headed to their rides. Mya and Juelz drove back to Mya's' house in silence. Mya and Juelz were driving down Winding Way and they saw 4 cop cars headed towards the Warehouse. Mya and Juelz played it cool and when the cops passed their car, they both looked through their rear-view mirrors to make sure that they were in the clear. Mya turned the corner and suddenly remembered that neither she nor Juelz had wiped off the outside doorknob of the Warehouse's front door.

Mya looked at Juelz and said, "Yo, I just thought about something. Neither of us wiped the doorknob off to the front Warehouse door".

Juelz looked at Mya and answered, "Don't worry about that yo. I didn't use my bare hand to open the door".

Mya felt a huge sense of relief and looked at Juelz and said, "That's why I love you boo. You always thinking on ya toes".

As Mya and Juelz were headed to her house, her overthinking started to get the better of her. Mya asked herself, "I wonder if we actually wiped everything off and got everything out of there that had our name on it? I find it kinda strange that when I told Juelz that I loved him, he said always and forever, just like sneaky link 2 always says to me."

As usual, Mya's thoughts were interrupted by her arriving at home and pulling up into the driveway. Juelz jumped out of the car and went to pull up the garage door manually. As soon as Juelz closed the garage door, he jumped back into the car with Mya because he wanted some personal answers from Mya before the rest of the gang showed up. When Juelz jumped back into the car, Mya could tell by the way that he slammed his door, that he was going to ask Mya something that she was going to have to lie about.

Juelz took a deep breath and as he was staring out the front windshield he said to Mya, "Yo. Is there something that you gotta tell me?"

Mya had already made up her mind that she wasn't going to give up the tapes.

Mya also stared out the window as she answered Juelz. "No Juelz".

Juelz knew that Mya was lying so he angrily jumped out of the car, slammed the door, stood in the garage, and sparked a wood.

Mya knew that he was in his feelings, and she decided to just walk into the house and not irk him anymore. As Mya got out of the car and headed to the garage door that led to the kitchen, Juelz received a FaceTime call from the Brothers.

"Yizzo", answered Juelz.

Mya quickly said to Juelz, "Could you tell everyone to pull around back and park in the garage driveway and the grass?"

The brothers heard Mya and they answered, "Copy".

Mya thought Juelz was out of his feelings by the way he answered that call, so she decided to say something to him. Mya headed over to Juelz, grabbed him from behind, and rested her head on his back.

She started to cry and softly whispered, "I'm sorry Juelz".

Juelz was obviously still in his feelings because he did not respond to her, she became upset when she saw that she didn't get the reaction that she was looking for from him, so she angrily yanked her arms from around his waist and started to speed walk into the house. Juelz turned towards Mya and waved her off and then the Brothers' secret knock could be heard on the garage door. Juelz went over to open the door and the Warriors and brothers were all laughing and joking as they came into the garage, but they could all see that Juelz looked vexed and Mya was crying. While Mya was still crying, she looked at the gang and ran into the house. Juelz put out the wood and sucked his teeth as he ran behind Mya.

The Warriors and Brothers all looked at each other and said, "Trouble in paradise yet again."

Steph looked at Skyler and said, "Stay outta that shit gang".

Steph was Skyler's man and although their relationship was off and on, they apparently were 'a thing' again. One thing about Sklyer is that she did not play with Steph. She respected that nigga when they were together, and his word was law. Skyler and Steph headed into the house and went straight to the basement.

Jihad was the last one to enter the garage and he went over to hit the automatic sensor that closed the garage door. He hit it a few times and Juelz could hear that he was banging on the sensor from where he was in the kitchen.

Juelz yelled out to Jihad, "You have to grab the handle up top and pull that jawn down". "Wait, wait, wait," Asia yelled to Jihad.

"Let me go grab that red velvet cake out the trunk."

Asia then looked at Yao and said, "Babe, could you come with and grab the case of Heineken out the backseat?"

Yao followed behind Asia, and as Yao was walking out of the garage, he looked at Jihad and said, "You think that you can handle grabbin' the handle?"

Jihad looked at Yao and said, "Whateva nigga. Just gone handle ya fucking business and I'll handle mine."

While Jihad waited in the garage, he and Ktru started kissing and feeling up on each other.

"Eww, get a room", Asia said as she was coming back into the garage.

As Yao followed behind, Jihad could be seen jumping up three times and he couldn't grab the garage door handle.

Yao looked at Jihad and jokingly said, "Need some help with that lil guy?"

"Whateva nigga. Ya dick ain't bigger than mine though", Jihad answered.

Steph and Skyler were already down in the basement, Mya and Juelz were over in the kitchen corner arguing and everyone else headed down to the basement except Asia and Yao.

"Why the fuck is you always fuckin' playin wit me, Mya?" Juelz screamed at her as he yoked Mya up in the corner. Asia and Yao immediately ran over to break them up.

"Come on man. We got shit to do, plus that shit ain't cool", Yao said to Juelz as he was pulling him away from Mya.

Although Juelz was fiery hot because he thought Mya was trying to play him, Mya was sexually turned on because she got aroused when Juelz manhandled her.

Julez could see that Mya was turned on and he said to Asia and Yao, "Look at her crazy ass! This is exactly the fuck what she wants me to do. She like this shit!"

Yao managed to pull Juelz off of Mya and he and Juelz headed down to the basement. While they were walking into the basement, Yao said to Juelz, "man, you really gotta chill wit putin ya hands on her. That shit ain't cool bro".

Juelz looked Yao straight in the eyes and coldly said, "That bitch keep playin' wit me. She gone have me kill her dumbass".

Yao paused on the step and looked at Juelz like he was crazy as Juelz nonchalantly walked down the steps and headed over to the rest of the crew.

Asia and Mya were still in the kitchen corner talking.

Asia looked at Mya and said, "Sis, what is really going on with you?"

Mya looked at Asia and started crying as she whispered, "I think I might be pregnant".

Asia grabbed her chest in shock as she covered her mouth in disbelief, then said, "OMG, you told us that you were a no entry, virgin!"

Mya looked at Asia and said, "Bitch be for real".

Asia then started to do what Asia is known for doing, thinking rationally and trying to solve the problem.

Asia asked Mya, "ok, ok, ok. What makes you think that you may be pregnant?"

Mya then answered, "I am always throwing up, all times of the day, for no reason and as you can see, I am mad moody".

Asia then said, "Have you told Juelz yet? Are you planning to keep the baby?"

Mya sighed deeply then answered, "To be honest, I haven't really thought about what I am going to do. Plus, I haven't even taken a pregnancy test".

Mya then went on to say, "Please, please, please don't say anything to ANYONE else about this until I am 100% sure".

Asia looked at Mya, smiled, and hugged her. As they rocked back and forth, Asia jokingly said to Mya, "Don't worry. You know God Mommie got your back."

They both laughed and Mya said, "whateva bitch".

CHAPTER 9

Mya and Asia headed to the basement and Asia was wiping the tears from Mya's face. Asia whispered to Mya, "You gotta pull it together or they gone know something's up".

Mya shook it off and started being dramatic as she walked into the basement with the rest of the gang. The basement was filled with smoke and different conversations going on among the Warriors and Brothers. Everybody and their "partners" were seated next to each other. Rainah and Rock were hugged up on the loveseat. Jihad and Ktru were standing over by the pool table. Steph and Skyler were playing dominoes. Yao was sitting on the couch hitting the vape pen and Juelz was in the game chair playing the PS-5 and talking on the phone.

Asia walked over to the couch, jumped on Yao and Mya could see that Juelz was high-key trying to piss her off by ignoring that she was now in the basement.

Mya in her petty fashion, loudly yelled out, "AHEM. I need EVERYONE'S attention because we got shit to do!"

The gang already knew that Mya was being petty with Juelz, so they all came closer together so that this drama would not drag out. Juelz was side-eyeing Mya as he whispered something to whomever he was on the phone with and then spun the chair around to face the rest of the gang.

They all sat around in silence and Mya said, "Well since no one else is starting, I guess I'll go".

Mya took a deep breath and then said, "Long story short. I peeped the Chevy on my street this morning when the Warriors came to the house to pick me up for school, then this same car came from outta nowhere and tried to run us off the fucking road. We also peeped the Chevy in the McDonald's parking lot by the High and then there's that bull shit that popped off at the Warehouse".

Rock asked, "Do any of ya'll know anything about who it may be and why the fuck they targeting y'all?"

Mya looked around and said, "Well, the streets told me that the Chevy belongs to some nigga named Pooh and supposedly his car was jacked".

Jihad looked at the brothers and asked, "Do any of y'all niggas know who this cat is?"

Steph answered, "Nah nigga. I ain't neva heard nuthin' bout this clown".

Mya was secretly looking at Juelz, peeping at his body language and she could tell that he was about to say some dumb shit.

Juelz looked and Mya and then said, "Nah nigga. The real question is, who the fuck even told you bout this Pooh nigga?"

Everyone sucked their teeth and started to yell out random things in response to Juelz's jealous, petty ass comment.

"Aw, come on man", Rock said.

Ktru then asked, "Who the fuck was bussin in the Warehouse?"

The Brothers all shrugged their shoulders and then Yao said, "you know we wouldn't even bring no heat to a place where we set shit up".

Skyler looked around and could see that everyone was getting off track and she said, "aight y'all. So, the Brothers are going to handle finding out who this Pooh nigga is, but we all need to decide what we going to do for the rest of the night. The night is mad young, and it's my bitches birthday!"

Rainah played some music, and it was, Spiffy the Goat's, "Throw it".

Asia was the first one to jump up and Mya made her way to the middle of the basement, as the Warriors circled around her and they started clapping and singing the song, "You don't need no crowd, you betta hype ya bestie up".

Mya danced in the middle of the circle and Ktru screamed out, "Alright birthday bitch, go get yaself together so that we all can head down to The Square ".

The Square was a popular underage, legit spot where all the area High School teens went on the weekend, to turn up.

Mya answered, "I'm down, but I need about 15-20, to get myself together".

The Warriors all yelled, "Well go handle that bitch. We on go mode!"

Mya headed up the stairs and the rest of the gang peeped that Juelz was about to follow her upstairs.

Everybody randomly started talking shit. Rainah yelled out, "Awww shit. Somebody bout to get some birthday yams!"

The Warriors all laughed, and Mya yelled back, "whateva bitch!"

Juelz followed Mya up the steps and the Warriors and their on again, off agains', continued smoking and dancing with one another. Mya got midway up the stairs, where she could no longer be seen by the others, and she started to enticingly pop her ass in front of Juelz. Juelz ran up behind her, bit her on the ass cheek, and picked her up from behind. Mya loved that rough shit and Juelz knew it. Juelz put Mya down when they got into the kitchen and immediately, they started going at it. Juelz threw Mya up against the refrigerator and Mya pushed Juelz back so that his ass landed up against the kitchen counter. Mya aggressively unbuckled his pants, pulled them down along with his briefs, dropped down on both of her knees, and ate the dick.

Mya deepthroated all 7 1/2 inches of Juelz's dick, then took it out her mouth, and spat on it, as she looked up at Juelz with spit all over her mouth and chin.

Juelz looked down at Mya and said, "damn, I fuckin' love you to death girl. You so fuckin' nasty".

Mya's slurps and gawk sounds filled the kitchen along with Juelz's moans.

Mya was double-twisting, licking, sucking, and slurping on the dick and Juelz couldn't take it any longer. He was about to cum. Mya could taste Juelz's pre cum and as she was handling her business she whispered, "I want you to cum in my mouth".

Juelz grabbed Mya's braids from the back of her head and started quickly pushing her head forward so that his dick went deeper down her throat. 'Gwak, gwak, gwak' and gag sounds were heard from Mya, as she kept doing the same hand work, although Juelz was pushing her head down all crazy on the dick.

"Oh shit, oh shit, ooooooo shhhhhhiiiiiiit! Juelz cried out as he bussed in Mya's mouth.

He looked down at Mya and she looked at Juelz as she swallowed the last bit of Juelz's cum. Mya spit some back on his dick and then sucked his dick clean. Juelz paused and looked Mya dead in her eyes and said, "God damn babe. You betta not be doing this shit to nobody else bitch".

Mya didn't respond, she just licked all around her mouth, making sure that she didn't waste a drip drop. Juelz took his semi-stiff dick and playfully started slapping it on Mya's face.

Mya got up off her knees, pressed her body against Juelz's body, and tried to tongue-kiss him.

Juelz jerked his head back and said, "Come on yo. You know I don't even play dem type of games".

Mya said, "Alright den. Imma head upstairs, brush my teeth, do a quick STP (Slits, tits, and pits) wash, and then I'mma be ready".

"Coo", Juelz answered. Mya headed up the kitchen stairs that led to the back of the house and when she got to the 3rd step, something told her to keep stomping on the 3rd step to make Juelz think that she was headed upstairs, however she would still be on the 3rd step. Mya got really quiet and listened to see what Juelz's next move would be. Juelz could be heard dialing on his cell. Mya made sure to be really still and remain quiet as a mouse.

Juelz could be heard whispering on the phone, "Yo. What it do sun?"

Mya could not hear the voice on the other line, so she did not know if it was a guy or a girl because Juelz called everyone sun. Mya tried her hardest, but she could not make out what Juelz was saying, so she just waited on the steps until he could be heard heading back down into the basement.

It wasn't long before Mya heard Juelz walking down the basement stairs. Mya waited until she heard everyone downstairs start talking their shit to him then she headed up the backstairs. Mya walked towards her room and as she was about to walk into the bathroom, she received a text message. The text message was from an unknown person and the text read, "Everything ain't always what it seems".

Mya went to another place in her room where she kept her secret liquor stash, pulled out a 5th of Henny, and started to chug it. After she was done sippin', she remembered that she had to go back into Genie's room and put the keys back where she found them. Just as she opened Genie's door, she was receiving a call from Genie.

Mya took a breath, collected herself, and then answered, "Hey Genie! Is we rich?"

Genie chuckled and then said, "Chile, hell no. I ain't doing nuthin' but winnin' my money back".

Mya could tell that Genie had something on her mind, so Mya said, "I heard from Mychelle today. She was callin' to check up on me she wished me a happy birthday".

Genie answered, "Humph. How she doin? She don't seem to call me much lately".

Mya told Genie that she was doing okay and then Genie said, "Some of these old bats round here talkin' about some riff-raff that happened at the Warehouse this evening. You wouldn't happen to know anything about that would you?"

Mya acted shocked and she replied, "No Genie, I haven't heard anything".

"Um humph", Genie replied as if she already knew that Mya was lying. "Anyway, I was jus calling to tell you that I ain't going to be home tonight, but don't think that this is an invitation for you to be actin' a fool".

"Genie I'm not. The Warriors are going to come over, we gone hang out in the basement and then they gone sleepover".

"Alright now. You know I got eyes and ears everywhere chile", Genie said.

"I know, I know", Mya answered. They disconnected from the call and Mya carefully walked into Genie's room to put the keys to The Bucket, back where she found them.

Mya headed back to her room and took her little bird bath. Mya already had her birthday fit out on her desk chair, and as she was undressing, Juelz came through the door.

Juelz looked at Mya and said, "You ready babe? The gang is ready to move".

Mya continued to get dressed as Juelz watched her. Mya was still feeling some type of way about that sus call that Juelz had made earlier in the kitchen, so she said, "Sheesh, can a bitch get some privacy?"

Juelz blew Mya off and said, "Are you being serious right now? I know, remembered, and have seen, every inch of your body".

Mya didn't feel like getting into it with Juelz, so she quietly finished getting dressed. After Mya got dressed, Juelz looked at her and said, "damn birthday girl. You threw that shit on, huh?"

Although Mya was mad at Juelz, the way he made her feel was addicting.

CHAPTER 10

ya blushed, although she didn't want to. Juelz then pulled out some white girl. "Here birthday girl. Lemme git you right before I have to go out and share you with the world".

Mya hesitated because she wasn't sure if she was pregnant or not, then she thought to herself, "hell, I been smoking and drinking, so what the fuck? will taking a bump or two, make a difference?"

Mya took two bumps and on her last bump, Juelz pushed Mya forward onto her bed. Juelz then said to Mya, "Get on your knees and slide your pretty ass back here to the edge of the bed".

Mya did exactly what Juelz said, and she already knew what was about to go down, so she immediately started to cream.

Julez pulled Mya's thong to the side, squatted down, and spit in her ass.

Mya thought that Juelz was about to slowly slide his dick into her, however, her asshole was greeted by a warm, stiff, and wet tongue.

Mya screamed out in pleasure. "Oh my god Juelz. What the fuck is you trynna do to me?" Mya asked between her loud moans.

Juelz roughly started to smack Mya's ass cheeks, while sucking her ass and then he gently slid his finger into her asshole and started stroking it. Juelz was able to taste and feel the creaminess of Mya's pleased, dripping pussy. Juelz started to make slurping sounds in her asshole. Juelz then gently slid 2 fingers into her pussy, he took his fingers out of her pussy and sucked the creaminess off. He could feel Mya's pussy walls tighten and he knew that she was about to cum.

Juelz felt Mya's body trembling and then all of a sudden, he jumped up, slapped Mya on the ass and said, "Alright yo. We gotta go". Mya plopped down face-first onto her bed with major disappointment.

"Juelz are you fucking serious my nigga?" She yelled.

Juelz looked at Mya, licked his lips, and said, "Come on babe. On some real shit. We gotta slide".

Mya jumped up off her bed, pulled her thong back where it belonged, and said, "Coo. I want you to keep that same energy".

Mya and Juelz headed downstairs, and she was angry and turned on at the same time, about the bullshit that Juelz had just pulled. Mya received a FaceTime call from Rainah letting her know that the Warriors were all in the SUV waiting for her and the Brothers were in the G-Wagon, waiting for Juelz.

Julez knew that Mya was pissed off, so right before they headed outside, Juelz seductively grabbed Mya by the neck and tongue-kissed the shit out of her.

"You get on my fucking nerves," Mya said as Juelz softly bit her bottom lip.

Mya and Juelz headed out to get into their rides and while Mya was walking to the SUV, Skyler yelled out the window at Mya "okkkk. I see you bitch".

Mya did a little model catwalk then she posed.

Juelz looked at Mya and said, "Yeah. don't let them get you fucked up outchea tonight".

Mya waved Juelz off and went to get into the front passenger seat. Juelz was watching Mya as she walked away and then Mya bent over so that Juelz could see that she had taken her thong off. Juelz sucked his teeth and slammed the garage door shut and then mumbled to himself, "I swear to god this bitch irks my fucking soul".

Juelz hopped in the back of the G-Wagon and Rock, who was the driver, stuck his arm out the window and made a hand gesture that told the Warriors to follow behind them. Rock pulled off and Mya played 'Outside' by Beatking. The Warriors all started screaming along with the song, "bitch we outside tonight!"

Mya hit the sunroof button to open the sunroof, stood up so that the top half of our body was outside and then Asia reached up front and started smacking Mya's ass as she was twerking. Mya was halfway out of the sunroof, still singing along with the song, as they drove down the street. Rainah could see that the Brothers were looking at them through the rearview and then Ktru yelled out, "Let's race those niggas". Ktru rolled down her window,

Skyler rolled down her window and they both started banging on the outside of the SUV. "Go, go, go, go!" they yelled to Rainah.

Rainah pulled alongside the Brothers looked over at Rock and sped off in front of them.

Asia yelled out, "Yeah niggas".

The Warriors were zooming down Ace Street and then all of a sudden, the Brothers whizzed past them. "Awww shit, Ktru said. "These niggaz want all the smoke Rainah!" Raniah put the pedal to the medal as the Warriors were hyping her up. Just as Rainah had reached the rear of the G-Wagon, Rock skeeted off on them like the mutherfucka was driving a hell cat.

Mya was still hanging out of the window yelling, "Git they assess Rainah. Let them niggas see what this Beamer can do!" Rainah put the BMW into sport mode and the SUV jerked and then the upper half of Mya's body was being flung back and forth while she was outside the sunroof. "Un unh bitch, Mya said. Let me sit my goofy ass down".

Rainah passed the Brothers and as the Warriors were dustin' them off, Mya, Ktru, and Skyler put their arms outside of the window and stuck up their middle fingers.

Mya was also singing, "Bitch we outside tonight", while passing them. Rainah made a sharp turn onto Progress Street and headed towards Kale Boulevard, where The Square was located. Asia turned around to see if the Brothers were behind them and then out of nowhere, the Brothers pulled into the parking lot right before the Warriors did.

As the Warriors and Brothers were jumping out of their rides, Rock said to Rainah, "I told you babe that it ain't always about speed. You gotta have them fuckin' skills my boy!"

Rainah looked at Rock and playfully stuck out her tongue and said, "An-tee-way!"

Rock put his arm around Rainah pulled her close to him and said, "You know I still love you though? Even though your skills is trash."

Everyone started laughing as they made their way into the club.

The Warriors and the Brothers were going through the front door and Juelz pulled

Mya back as she walked in. "What do you want, Juelz?"

Mya asked. Juelz looked at Mya and said, "Don't git in here and be actin' like no muthafuckin' fool".

Mya snatched away from Juelz's grip and answered, "Whateva nigga!"

Mya started speed walking so that she could catch up to the rest of the Warriors. As Mya was walking, she heard Juelz yell from the background, "I ain't fuckin' playin' Mya. Don't fuck around and find out!"

Mya ignored Juelz and went to catch up with her girls. Asia saw that Mya was right behind her and so she interlocked arms with Mya and said, "that nigga actin' nutty again?" "You already!" Mya answered. The Square was an underage club, so they did not sell any alcohol, but that definitely didn't stop the teens from having some on deck. The only thing is that if security caught someone drinking, they would be kicked out.

Mya pulled a bottle of water out of her tote bag and took a sip of the Vodka that she had put in it, to replace the water. Mya passed the water bottle to Skyler and Skyler looked at her and said, "unt unh bitch. I don't know where your mouth been?"

Mya twisted the cap back onto the water bottle and replied, "yea. You right", and they both started laughing.

The Warriors headed over to the dance floor and Mya told them that she had to pee. The girls usually didn't let each other go to the bathroom alone, however Mya told them that she was good. Mya wanted to go to the bathroom alone to take a few bumps, and the Warriors did not know that she did coke. As Mya headed to the bathroom, she suddenly was thrown up against the wall and had no idea what was happening. Mya thought to herself, *'this shit gotta stop. I need to git on my shit!'*. Mya spun around and was deeply tongue-kissed by Sneaky Link #1

CHAPTER 11

"W hat the fuck is you doing here?", Mya angrily asked as she pushed them away from her.

"You know that I wasn't going to miss my baby girl's birthday", the link answered. Mya was walking away to go into the bathroom and the link pulled her back. Mya yanked out of their grip and said, "I can't do this shit with you tonight yo! Juelz and his boys is here". "Man fuck them clown ass niggas", the link said.

Mya stuck up her middle finger and walked into the bathroom. Mya was in the bathroom stall and heard Ktru come in looking for her.

"Mya girl. You alright in here?" Ktru asked.

"Yea bitch. I'm good. I'm bout to come out now", Mya answered.

Mya put her coke away and walked out of the bathroom stall. Ktru was in the mirror fixing her makeup and said to Mya as they looked at each other through the mirror, "You know I saw your link in here tonight? Don't get no fuckin' shit started up in hea".

Ktru was the only one who knew about Sneaky Link 1.

Mya was fixing her lip gloss and she said to Ktru, "Girl, ain't nobody worried about these niggas."

Ktru turned to face Mya and said, "bitch look at me." Mya turned to face Ktru and Ktru said, "I'm for real bitch. You know that both of them niggas is nutty and none of us need any smoke, on top of this shit we already got shit going on with this fuckin Chevy!"

Mya kissed Ktru on the cheek and said, "Trust me boo. It's all good. I got this. Now let's go out there and properly celebrate my muthafuckin' birthday!"

Mya followed behind Ktru as they were leaving the bathroom and Mya smacked Ktru on the ass and said, "Good googly moogly!"

They both started laughing, interlocked arms, and headed towards the dance floor. The rest of the Warriors were already out in the middle of the dance floor and as Mya and Ktru were approaching them, the Warriors started yelling, "Bitch, throw that ass in a circle!" Mya started twerking and they all took turns smacking Mya on the ass.

The Warriors were all on, in the middle of the dance floor and having the time of their lives, and then all of a sudden, who comes over to hate on them? The fucking Valley Chicks. The leader of the pact started with the smoke. "

If it isn't Ms. Big Booty Judy. I guess you look kinda hot. In a stank way".

Mya twerked on Chloe and said, "That ain't what ya white boy think!"

The Warriors started laughing and then Ktru said, "Keep walking bitches because we ain't in school. We gone give y'all what the fuck y'all want".

The Valley Chicks answered in their white girl voices, "Whatever", and they all walked away.

Skyler screamed out, "we bout to go live on the Gram bitches!"

Skyler started recording the Warriors as The Valley Chicks were walking towards the bar to grab some water. Mya was coming up from her twerk, and she turned around to see that Chloe was grinding all up on Juelz.

Mya tweaked and said, "I know this nigga ain't!"

Juelz knew that these bitches were the Warriors' rivals. Mya pulled down her dress and headed towards their direction.

Ktru immediately grabbed Mya from behind and said, "Remember what I told you in the bathroom".

Mya stormed over to the bar to get a bottle of water and as she was sitting there cooling off, she spun her stool around to watch Chloe as she was grinding on Juelz.

Mya said to herself, "ok, that's how you wanna play nigga?".

Mya was finishing up her water, she looked over to the left and saw that sneaky link 1 was standing over on the wall, with his boys. Mya slammed the small water bottle down onto the bar and headed over to him. As Mya was approaching, sneaky link started licking his lips.

"Damn babe. I didn't know you was looking that fuckin' good!"

Sneaky link spun Mya around and as Mya turned her ass towards him, she bent over and started slowly grinding on him. Sneaky link licked his lips as he was looking down at her ass. Mya could feel his dick starting to get hard.

"Damn girl", he said.

Mya looked back at him and just as she was turning back around, Juelz came over and hooked off on the sneaky link.

Mya started screaming, "Juelz what the fuck is you doing yo? Ain't nobody do nothing when that white bitch was grindin all up on you!"

Sneaky link locked up with Juelz and threw him up against the wall and started giving him body shots.

The rest of the Brothers were trying to push through the crowd to make it over to Juelz, but before they could get there, sneaky link boys started jumping Juelz. The crowd wasn't moving out of the way fast enough, so Jihad pulled out his strap and shot 2 times into the air. The crowd started screaming, yelling and running in different directions. The Warriors already knew what was going on, so they ran over where the Brothers were in order to get to Mya. Mya was over there trying to pull sneaky link's homies off of Juelz. The Brothers finally made it over there and they all started mixing. Ktru grabbed Mya by the arm, yanked her and tried to get her to come outside. Mya yanked away from Ktru and said, "No fuck that". The Warriors all picked Mya up to carry her outside and as they were heading out, security rushed past them to get over to the brawl.

The Brothers were cool with security, so security was yanking them other niggas up, and telling the Brothers to get the fuck out of dodge. The Brothers got the fuck out of dodge because they knew it wouldn't be long before 12 showed up. As they were running outside to get in their ride, Mya was outside doing the most. The Warriors had no idea why Mya was tweaking, but it was the coke that had her doing the most. The Warriors tried everything they could to get Mya into the SUV.

"No, no. Get the fuck off of me, bitches. I ain't going nowhere. I'm waiting on this nigga!" Mya yelled.

Jihad said to the Warriors, "git y'all asses in the car and we'll meet up wit y'all at Mya's spot!"

Juelz ignored Mya's drama and ran past her to hop in the G-ride. Mya ran up behind Juelz and punched him in the back of his head.

"Oh, now you wanna ignore me nigga?" Mya said. Juelz turned around and smacked the shit out of Mya.

"Yo nigga. What the fuck is you doing?", Yao said to Juelz as he pushed Juelz towards the G-ride.

"That shit ain't cool gang", Steph said.

"Let's go nigga's", Rock ordered.

The Brothers hopped in the ride and Rock yelled out to Rainah, "get the fuck in the car and get the fuck outta here now!"

The Warriors hopped in the SUV and Mya was crying and holding her cheek as she headed to the SUV.

"I can't believe this nigga put his fucking hands on me", Mya said through her tears.

The Warriors were all silent because they did not know what to say. As they were driving down the Ave, the Warriors noticed that they were not too far behind the Brothers. Out of thin air, the black Chevy swerved out in front of the Warriors and sped up to the Brothers G-Wagon.

"Oh, my god, oh my god", Rainah yelled and started blowing her horn all crazy, trying to let the Brothers know that something was up.

CHAPTER 12

ock looked through his rear-view mirror and peeped that the black Chevy was driving mad crazy behind him. Rock started to speed up and the Chevy's engine could be heard revving. The Chevy pulled alongside the G-Wagon started to swerve over into its lane and hit the side of the jeep. Rock swerved back over into the lane of the Chevy and hit the side of the Chevy. This went on for about 1 mile before Jihad was seen rolling down his window, sticking out his gun, and firing 3 shots at the Chevy. The Chevy hit the G-Wagon one last time and then sped off. The last impact was so powerful that it made the G-Wagon spin-off in circles. When the car stopped spinning, Rock slammed on the breaks and then Rainah pulled over in front of them.

All of the Warriors immediately jumped out of the SUV except Mya.

Rainah ran straight over to the driver's side and said, "Oh my god baby! You, ok?" Rock slowly got out of the car and said, "Yeah babe, I'm straight."

The rest of the Brothers got out of the jeep.

"Y'all niggas straight?" Steph asked.

"We all good," Jihad answered.

The Brothers and the Warriors all started hugging their partners as Juelz made his way over to Rainah's BMW.

"Aye yo. Be coo," Yao screamed to Juelz.

Juelz ignored Yao and kept walking towards the BMW. Mya was still in the backseat crying and Juelz looked through the window and asked her, "You alright yo?"

Mya didn't answer Juelz, so he hopped in the backseat with her. Juelz started gently kissing Mya all over her face and said, "Babe, I am so sorry."

Mya sat there in silence while Juelz continued to kiss all over her face. "Babe, you know how I feel about your ass, and when I saw you wit' your ass all up on that nigga, I just lost it. I promise I will never put my hands on you again." Juelz turned Mya's head to face him and then he said, "On my momma, I promise you I will never do no shit like that again." Juelz softly kissed Mya on the lips and Mya slowly kissed him back. After they finished kissing, Juelz wiped the tears from Mya's face and then he softly whispered, "do you forgive me?" Mya blankly looked at him, stared down at the floor, and shook her head yes. Juelz continued to slowly and gently kiss Mya and then he said to her, "Tell me you love me."

Mya stared at Juelz for a minute and then she whispered, "I love you."

Juelz wrapped his arms around Mya and said, "Always and forever." Mya sank into his hug and started crying.

While they were sitting in the car, Rock came over and tapped the hood, and said to them, "come on yo, we gotta git the fuck outta here."

Juelz kissed Mya one last time and said, "I'll see you at your crib babe."

Mya didn't respond. She just softly threw her head back up against the seat. Before the Warriors came back to the truck, Mya quickly took 2 bumps. As she was finishing up, the Warriors were getting in the truck. Mya sniffed so that she could feel the drip and plus she knew that this wouldn't seem sus because the Warriors knew that she had been crying.

Asia jumped in the back and hugged Mya. "You ok friend?" Mya shook her head yes and then rested her head on Asia's shoulder.

The Warriors drove back to Mya's place in complete silence and the Brothers followed behind them.

As they were pulling up to Mya's house, Skyler said, "I don't know about y'all, but I just want to go to a telly, get in a hot shower, and relax."

"I feel that," said Ktru.

The plan was that they all were supposed to sleep over at Mya's. Considering the night they just had, Mya totally was feeling everyone going to hotels. The rest of the Warriors went to hotels because they wanted to be alone with their men. They all had already told their families that they were staying the night with Mya, so there wouldn't be any parent beef. The Brothers finally pulled up to Mya's house.

Skyler turned around and looked at Mya then asked, "You sure you want to be alone with Juelz tonight?"

Mya looked back at Skyler and said, "Yea, sis I'm good."

The Warriors all got out of Rainah's SUV and started hugging one another and telling each other to be safe.

"Alright y'all. Text a bitch when y'all have checked into the hotel," Mya said.

"Will do," Skyler answered.

The gang all started pulling off and Juelz gently put his arm around Mya as they walked towards the garage. Juelz pulled up the garage door for Mya and then slammed the door shut.

"How is it safe that you can just open that garage door without the key?" Juelz asked Mya.

Mya kept walking and answered, "the garage key has a sensor in it, and you can't open or close the door unless you have the garage key close by."

Mya nonchalantly walked inside and headed upstairs.

Juelz said to Mya, "Babe you hungry?" Mya didn't answer and kept walking upstairs.

Juelz followed behind Mya and was holding her ass as she walked up the stairs. Mya didn't know how to feel. She was angry, confused, disappointed, scared, and turned on, all at the same time. Mya walked into her room, slowly pulled off her clothes, and went to hop in the shower. "Babe, I'mma UberEats us some grub from the Chinese joint on Vacant Way. You want your usual?"

Mya shrugged her shoulders and she headed into her bathroom. Mya turned the shower water on and while the water was running, she looked at herself in the mirror, turned her face to the left, and she could see that there was a black and blue mark on her cheek, and it was a little swollen. Mya pulled out some coke, took 3 bumps, and started crying. Juelz had finished ordering their grub and he heard Mya in the bathroom trying to softly cry.

Juelz walked into the bathroom, went over to Mya, turned her around, and started gently kissing her neck. Mya wasn't feeling him at all, and Juelz could tell, so he took all of his clothes off and pressed his body up against her. As they stood there naked, Juelz looked at Mya's face and could see what he had done to her.

"Fuck! Baby. I can't believe I did that dumb ass shit to you. I am so fucking sorry that I hurt you and made you feel unsafe. I know nothing that I say or do, will change the way you are feeling. All I am asking of you is your sincere forgiveness, Mya. Please tell me that you forgive me, baby. Please don't leave me, Mya." Mya stared Juelz in the eyes and said, "I forgive you, big dad."

Juelz picked Mya up and Mya wrapped her legs around his waist. They were kissing deeply and passionately as Juelz carried her inside of the shower. Juelz gently threw Mya up against the shower wall, slowly stuck his dick inside of her, and began to passionately make love to her.

Juelz and Mya hadn't fucked in about a month and by the way, both of their bodies reacted, they both could tell that they missed each other.

"Damn, baby. This pussy is so fucking tight!" Juelz moaned.

Mya tried to still be mad at Juelz, but it felt too good for her to front. Mya started to roughly kiss Juelz on the neck as he stroked and bounced her up and down.

"Oh, my fucking god. This shit is so fucking good babe," Juelz said.

Juelz moans got louder, and his dick went deeper, and Mya could feel that Juelz was bussin' inside of her. "I fucking love you," Mya said as she was cumming.

Mya could feel that Juelz was also cumming inside her again and this shit turned her on even more. Juelz and Mya both screamed out in ecstasy, as they came together. After they came, Juelz stayed inside of Mya. Juelz placed his head on her shoulder and enjoyed the feeling of the shower water beating down on his back. Juelz and Mya stayed in this position for about one minute and Mya started kissing on Juelz's necks. Mya tightened her pussy walls like she was doing kegel, and she could feel that Juelz's dick was getting hard again.

Juelz put Mya down, roughly turned her around, bent her over, and slowly and gently, slid his dick inside of her ass. Juelz was about 3 deep strokes in and then he pulled out and bussed on her back. As Juelz was shaking the rest of the nut off onto Mya's back, Mya stood up and gently pushed Juelz to the side, so that she could get in the front of the shower and wash up.

"Damn babe, it's like that?" Juelz asked as he chuckled.

Juelz got out of the shower and said, "I'mma go check to see if our food got here yet. Mya finished showering and when she heard Juelz going down the steps, she quickly jumped out of the shower and headed to the bed and grabbed Juelz's phone. Mya knew that it would be unlocked because he had just ordered their food. Mya quickly grabbed her phone and started taking pictures of Juelz's incoming and outgoing calls. Mya did the same with some of his text messages. Right before Mya was about to toss his phone back on the bed, she noticed a number that she was familiar with, but the name was stored under unknown. She couldn't remember off top who it was. Mya heard Juelz coming back upstairs, so she tossed his phone back onto the bed.

Mya grabbed her lotion, sat in the chair on the opposite side of the bed where his phone was, and started putting lotion on her feet. Juelz sat the Chinese on the dresser and then put his briefs on.

Mya looked at him and said, "why did you go downstairs naked? What if Genie would have walked in?"

Juelz looked at Mya, stuck out his tongue, and started swinging his dick from side to side while saying, "Then Genie would understand why you can't leave me alone."

They both started laughing and they both received text message notifications. Mya picked up her phone and saw that it was the Warriors texting to let her know that they were all checked in. Mya replied, turned her phone face-side down, and then put it on her nightstand. Juelz, however, didn't send a reply to his text.

Mya and Juelz usually slept together naked, but she wasn't really feeling Juelz after what popped off tonight. Mya put on a night gown, sat up in the bed, and asked Juelz to pass her the food.

Juelz sat down beside her and then said, "I gotta find out who the fuck is driving that muthafucka Chevy."

Mya looked at Juelz and said, "babe, can we just eat, chill, watch a movie, and talk about this shit in the A.M.?"

Juelz looked at Mya, kissed her, and said, "respect." Juelz put on a hood flick, and they started eating. While they were eating and watching the movie, Juelz's phone kept vibrating. The first two times, Mya ignored it.

The third time, Mya finally said, "who the fuck is blowing you up this time of night?" Juelz didn't even make eye contact with Mya.

He sucked his teeth, waved his hand at his phone, and said, "that shit ain't bout nuthin."

Mya looked at Juelz and said, "you know what? I just lost my appetite."

CHAPTER 13

ya wrapped up her food, took her phone off of the nightstand, and headed into the bathroom. Mya thought that she was going to get a reaction from Juelz, but he didn't react. Mya went into the bathroom, shut the door, and sat down on the toilet. Mya went into her phone to look for those pictures she had taken from Juelz's phone. Mya started to put the phone numbers in an app that she had downloaded onto her phone. The app allowed paid users to have access to cell phone numbers. Mya started putting in the numbers and screenshotting the info. Mya was just about to enter another cell phone number, and Juelz burst through the bathroom door.

"What is taking you so long?" he asked Mya.

Mya sucked her teeth. Usually, Juelz would be acting all nutty, but Mya knew that he was trying not to make her feel unsafe.

Mya got up, wiped then washed her hands. "Don't start your shit Juelz," she said. Mya headed over to her bed, got under the covers, and said, "I'm going to sleep yo. I'm tired."

As Mya snuggled under the covers, Juelz got in the bed behind her and then pulled Mya close to him. Mya and Juelz dozed off to sleep and somehow, Mya's bad dream from earlier continued. Mya was being tossed off the balcony and then someone in a black hoodie appeared out of thin air. The hooded person shot each of the guys who were trying to toss her over the balcony, in the head. The unknown person who saved Mya, went over to Mya while she was on the ground, leaned over her, and asked if she was okay. This unknown person was just about to remove their hoodie from their head, then Mya woke up. Mya turned over to feel for Juelz and he wasn't in the bed.

Mya hit the lamp in her room, and she saw that all of Juelz's belongings were nowhere in sight. Mya already knew that he wouldn't be walking around the crib, but she checked the whole crib anyway. Mya put her robe and house slippers on and grabbed her phone to use the flashlight. Mya checked the whole house and there were no signs of Juelz. Mya became angry as fuck and so she FaceTimed Juelz. Mya called 3 times and he didn't answer. Mya tried one last time and on the last call, she could tell that the phone had been turned off because it went straight to voicemail. Mya became mad as hell, so she decided to leave a message.

"You know what Juelz? I am sick of your shit. You couldn't leave me a note, a text, something to let a bitch know that you were leaving? I swear on everything I fuckin' loved you. I AM FUCKIN' DONE wit' your nut ass!"

Mya hung up the phone and checked to see what time it was. The time was 3:00 A.M. and she knew it was too early to call the Warriors, so she called Sneaky Link 2.

"What do I owe the pleasure of you calling me this early," sneaky Link said.

"Can you come lay with me?" Mya asked.

"Be there in 20", sneaky link replied. Mya headed back up to her room and she noticed something strange in the kitchen. Genie's hanging flowerpot which hung next to the kitchen door leading to the garage, was broken. Soil and pot pieces were all over the kitchen floor.

"What the fuck?" Mya said as she went over to start picking up the pieces of the pot. Mya opened the door that led to the garage, and she noticed that the garage door was halfway open.

"What the fuck is going on?" she said to herself.

Mya went to close the garage door and before she could shut it, Sneaky Link 2 appeared at the back of the house.

"Damn, did you smell me coming?" sneaky link jokingly asked.

Mya sucked her teeth and said, "Whatever yo. I was checking on some shit."

Sneaky Link walked into the garage and as Mya was walking into the house, Sneaky Link pulled the garage door closed.

Mya turned around and said to sneaky link, "What the fuck? How in the hell did you know that you have to pull the garage door down?"

Sneaky Link paused, looked at Mya, and said, "Why you trippin' yo? I saw that you were putting it down by the handle as I was coming up to the crib". Mya looked confused and said, "yea ok".

They both walked into the house and as they were headed upstairs, sneaky Link said to Mya, "Hey, Imma meet you upstairs. I wanna grab something to drink real quick."

Mya didn't even bother to respond, she just headed up the kitchen stairs. When Mya got to the top of the stairs, she closed the hallway closet door, to make her sneaky link think that she had gone into her bedroom. Mya stood at the top of the stairs listening for what was going on down in the kitchen. Sneaky link was heard having a conversation with someone on FaceTime.

"Yo, I told you that I would call you. Why the fuck are you calling me?"

Mya could barely hear the voice on the other line, but she could tell that it was a man. The male voice answered, "I just wanted you to know that we received the package."

"Coo. I'll hit you up later in the A.M. and then I'll let you know the next move," the voice said. The call hung up and Mya quickly and quietly tiptoed into her room.

Mya was lying across her bed when Sneaky Link came into the bedroom. Mya noticed that Sneaky Link did not have a drink in their hand, but Mya didn't want to question them and cause them to be suspicious.

Sneaky Link laid down beside Mya and said, "So, what do I really owe the pleasure of being here at 3:30 in the morning?"

Mya answered, "I didn't want to be alone. Is there something wrong with that?" Sneaky Link looked at Mya and asked, "What's been up wit you lately? You've been mad moody, and honestly, it's been hard to be around ya ass."

Mya shrugged her shoulders and said, "I don't know. If I had to guess, that day you told me that info about my brother's possible murder, I ain't been right."

"I can dig it," Sneaky Link replied as they pulled Mya close to them.

As Mya and her sneaky link lay on the bed cuddling, Mya received a FaceTime call from an unknown number. Mya looked at the phone and said, "Who the fuck could this be calling me from an unknown number at this time in the morning? I'm not answering that shit." The FaceTime call came through about 2 more times before Mya finally decided to answer the call. As soon as Mya answered the call, you could see that it was Juelz, strapped to a chair with a gag in his mouth.

"Oh my god Juelz. Please don't tell me this is another one of y'all fucking surprises. It's too early in the morning for this shit!"

Someone wearing a mask that had big Xs for the eyes spoke with a robot-like voice. They went on to say, "I assure you that this is no prank." The masked person then pistol-whipped Juelz.

Mya remembered Juelz had always told her that she has to remain cool even in the most fucked up situations. Mya took a deep breath and then said, "What do you want?"

The person in the mask started to laugh and then answered, "I think that you are asking the wrong question."

Mya looked at her sneaky link and asked them, "What should I ask?"

Sneaky Link said to Mya, "Ask them why they took Juelz."

The masked person overheard Sneaky Link and laughed again, "Ah ha. Now we are getting somewhere."

The masked person was silent and then Mya asked, "Well are you going to answer the question?"

The masked person answered," That is not a question for me to answer. That is a question that you need to ask yourself," and then the call was disconnected.

CHAPTER 14

Mya and Sneaky Link (2) were in her bedroom, trying to figure out what the fuck was going on.

Sneaky Link started off by asking, "What the fuck is you and this nigga gittin' into?" Mya sat on the edge of her bed, with her head in her hands, and replied, "I swear, I don't know what the fuck is going on." Mya thought about what had popped off at the Square last night and said, "The only incident that I was in with Juelz, was last night at the Square." Sneaky Link looked at Mya and said, "ok, keep talkin'."

Mya was iffy on whether or not to share the information because if there was one thing that her brothers taught her, it was that you had to watch who you hand information to. Mya looked at Sneaky Link and said, "Honestly, I was so fuckin activated, that I don't really remember shit. The only thing that I remember is everyone screaming and running out of the building."

Sneaky Link already knew that Mya was cappin so they replied,

"Well, if you wanna be all secret squirrel and shit, I ain't got nuthin else to say about this shit."

Sneaky Link started to walk out of Mya's bedroom and Mya said, "Where the fuck are you going?"

Sneaky Link ignored Mya and continued to walk out of her room and headed downstairs. Mya silently followed Sneaky Link downstairs and as Sneaky Link was leaving, neither of them said anything to each other. Mya shut the door, slammed her body against the wall, slowly slid down the wall, and started crying. Mya sat on the floor crying for about five minutes. Mya checked the time, and it was already 7:00 in the morning. Mya knew that if not one, then all of the Warriors would be up. Mya group FaceTimed the Warriors and they answered with worry.

"Is everything ok bitch?" Ktru asked.

They could see that Mya had been crying and Rainah said, "Say less bitch." Rainah asked the rest of the Warriors if they could have themselves together and ready to go in an hour. The Warriors agreed that they would be ready by then.

"Coo. sit tight. We'll be there in about an hour," Rainah said to Mya. Mya was crying so much that she couldn't even speak, instead she just blew them a kiss and the Warriors hung up the call.

Mya was still sitting on the floor when she received a call from her mom. Two years ago, when Mykel was murdered, Mya's mom had checked herself into a mental institution. Mya's mom's name is

Milan and she had suffered a major psychotic break after losing Mykel. Mya and her mom's relationship bond was very strong. Mya's mom and dad had divorced about a year after Mya's mom checked herself into the institution. Mya is still upset that Micheal (her dad), had divorced her mom during her lowest time. Especially at a time when she really needed him the most. Mya's dad remarried and they chose to have their own family. Mya now has 3 younger, half-siblings and she does not really rock with them that much. Mya was glad that her mom was calling her at a time when she needed her the most. Mya answered the call and all she could do was start crying again.

Mya's mom knew how to handle Mya very well, although she had not been physically present in Mya's life for two years. Milan gave her time to cry and just waited patiently for Mya to tell her what was going on.

Mya finished crying and finally said, "Mom, I need you so much right now."

Milan said to Mya, "Baby, tell mamma what's on your heart?"

Mya was softly crying; however, she was able to speak clearly. Mya went on to say, "Honestly mamma, there is so much that has happened to me in the past day, that I don't even know where to start."

Milan took a deep sigh and said, "Well my love, my next visiting day is tomorrow morning. I'll call your daddy and tell him to bring you up here and then come back to pick you up."

Mya was very happy with that idea and her mom asked, "Have you heard from your sister? How has she been?" Mya's sister and mom's relationship became rocky when she checked herself into the institution. Also, there was a lot of custody drama between Genie and their dad. Genie was granted partial guardianship and 50/50 custody of Mya and all her sisters' and brothers'. The courts gave Mya and the triplets a choice of who they wanted to live with. Mykel and Mycheal chose to go live with their dad and Mychelle chose with Mya and the twins, and they went to live with Genie. Mya gave her mom an update of what was going on with her sister and in the middle of their conversation, the Warriors FaceTimed Mya to let her know that they were out front and about to park.

"Mamma, the Warriors are outside, so I have to go," Mya said.

"Ok, baby. I look forward to seeing you tomorrow. Remember my love, always go with your first mind. Don't you eva let nobody make you feel like you crazy.

"You hear me?" Milan said.

"I hear you mamma," Mya answered.

"OK beautiful, you be safe. I love you and I'll see you tomorrow," Mamma said.

Mya ended the call and the Warriors walked through the front door. Mya was still sitting on the floor, so the Warriors got on the floor and surrounded her.

"What's going on friend," Skyler asked.

Rainah then said, "Let's all head to the kitchen, make some hot chocolate, and then go up to your room and talk about it."

"Sounds good," Mya said as she let out a slight giggle.

The Warriors helped Mya up off the floor and headed into the kitchen. Right as they were entering the kitchen, Ktru immediately noticed that Genie's favorite hanging pot had been broken.

"What happened to Genie's flowerpot?" Ktru asked.

Mya looked at Ktru and said, "Trust me. I am going to tell y'all everything when we go upstairs."

The Warriors were all in the kitchen talking, joking, and sharing laughs as they made their hot chocolate. Suddenly, Genie came through the kitchen door that led from the garage. Genie had a love/hate relationship with the Warriors, so they never knew what type of time she was going to be on when she came around them.

"Morning Genie," The Warriors said together.

"Mo'nin y'all." Genie answered. Genie didn't say anything else as she walked up the kitchen stairs. When Genie could no longer be heard in the upstairs hallway, Skyler said, "Genie didn't even notice her flowerpot was broken. Looks like somebody knocked the dust off that pussy last night!"

The Warriors started to laugh as they grabbed their hot chocolate and headed to Mya's room. Mya's Pop-Pop died from throat cancer ten years ago. He actually died a week before Mya's mom gave birth to her 10-year-old twin brother and sister. Genie has not been the same since his death and she has no desire to remarry.

The Warriors gathered in Mya's room, and they all got comfortable in different places. Some were on the bed, on the floor, and on the sofa. Mya was getting ready to tell the Warriors about everything that popped off and then Mya remembered what her brothers told her. Mya also remembered the text that she received from the unknown number. Mya really wanted to share all of the goings on with the Warriors, but she chose to make chess moves.

Mya took a long, deep breath and said, "Ok here's the situation. Y'all already know what first popped off in the morning with the Chevy, so I don't need to get into those dets. Y'all remember when we were at lunch, and I left school. Well, I took a ride with a friend, and we also had a car chase with the Chevy." Mya's intuition told her not to share the information about the word being on the streets that Pooh had something to do with Mykel's murder.

Mya then went on to say, "Y'all all know that Juelz stayed the night with me last night and when I woke up at 3:00 in the morning, he was nowhere to be found. I came downstairs looking for them and that's when I saw that the flowerpot had been broken. I called my friend and asked them to come and be with me. When I opened the kitchen door to the garage, the garage door was halfway open. I was in the middle of closing the garage door and my friend showed up. Then lastly, I got a FaceTime call around 3:30 this morning, from an unknown number. When I answered the call, Juelz was strapped to a chair with a gag in his mouth. There was a person that was wearing a mask, and it had an Xs for the eyes. This person's voice was also disguised with a robot computer-like sound. Whoever this person is, also pistol-whipped Juelz right before they ended the call."

The Warriors were all just sitting there listening in disbelief.

Rainah finally said as she plopped her body back onto Mya's bed, "What in the entire fuck, is going on yo?"

The girls just sat around for a few minutes, blankly staring at one another and trying to figure shit out.

Skyler then said, "Have you heard from Juelz again since that call this morning?" Mya shook her head no.

Asia said, "Well, I know none of the Brothers got wind about this because none of them said anything to either of us when we left them at the telly this morning."

Ktru said, "Well, our next move is to call the Brothers and let them niggas know what's up."

Skyler FaceTimed Steph and when Steph answered, he could tell by the look on Skyler's face that there was something wrong.

"What's up bae?" he asked.

The Warriors gathered around Skyler so that they could be seen on the call.

Skyler then said, "We need you to add the rest of the Brothers to this call."

Steph added the Brothers to the call and Jihad answered, "Yizzo."

Steph looked at Skyler and said, "Alright yo. The floor is yours." Skyler told Mya to come closer so that she could be seen more than anybody else.

Mya got into position and said, "Long story short, Juelz stayed with me last night when I woke up at 3:00, he was nowhere to be found. I went downstairs and the garage door was halfway opened, and Genie's favorite flowerpot had been broken. Around 3:30, I got a FaceTime call from an unknown number. I answered the

FaceTime call and Juelz was strapped to a chair with a gag in his mouth. The person who showed themselves had a mask on and it had Xs in the place where the eyes should have been. They spoke with a robot computer-like voice and right before they hung up the call, they pistol-whipped Julez."

"What the fuck!!!!" Jihad yelled. Why the fuck didn't you call us this morning when this fuckin' shit happened yo?"

Ktru came to Mya's defense and said, "She has never dealt with anything like this Jihad, so she doesn't know what the right thing is to do."

"Man fuck all that!" Jihad said. Anything popping off wit our boy needs to be known. Muthafuck the time and day!"

Yao then said, "All alright yo. Calm the fuck down. Let's deal with the real issue and that is finding out who the fuck got our boy?"

Rock then said, "I'm bout to put my boots to the pavement and see what my folks know."

Yao said to the Warriors, "Aye yo. Right now, I want all y'all to go straight home from Mya's house. Make sure that each of y'all call us on FaceTime when y'all lease and we will remain on FaceTime until y'all make it home safely."

CHAPTER 15

The Warriors all gave a thumbs up and started to gather their things to leave. The call was disconnected and the Warriors, all hugged one another and said,

"be safe". Mya walked them out, kissed them on their cheeks and asked them to FaceTime her when they made it home. All the Warriors drove their own car, so Mya stood at the door and watched them as they safely made it to their rides. Mya waved goodbye and blew air kisses to them as they each pulled off. Mya was making her way upstairs and she received a call from an unknown number.

"Juelz?" Mya hopefully asked. It was the same robot computerlike voice that called at 3:30 this morning. "I want you to listen closely and follow my instructions to the letter. In 15 minutes, COME ALONE and meet me at the abandoned warehouse over on Job and Calendar Street. Do not bring your phone., do not let anyone know where you are going, and most importantly, make sure that you make it here in exactly 15 minutes."

"That's impossible. I have to come on foot and that's an easy 25-minute walk," Mya anxiously said.

The masked person answered, "15 minutes and counting. The time starts now. Tick, tock, tick, tock," and then they hung up the call.

Mya quickly ran up the stairs and headed straight towards Genie's room. Mya was so scared that she didn't even knock on Genie's door. Mya burst through the door, huffing and puffing. Genie was asleep and Mya scared the shit out of her.

"Chile what in the hell is wrong with your crazy ass! Busting in my goddamn room like you ain't got no sense!" Genie yelled.

Mya could hardly breathe as she said, "Genie, I really really need to borrow your car!" Genie looked at Mya with her eyes halfway open and said,

"now you know goddamn well I ain't lettin' you use my damn car". Mya looked at her Apple watch, sucked her teeth and then slammed Genie's door shut.

"And stop slammin' my goddamn door!" Genie yelled at Mya, as she darted down the back stairs. Mya had absolutely no clue on how she was going to make it there in time and all of a sudden, she remembered that her Pop-pop had brought Genie a motorized bike and she never rode it. Mya burst through the kitchen door that led to the garage and then she went over towards the toolshed. Mya started tossing all the things from around the hidden bike. Mya grabbed the bike, went through the kitchen door and made her way out the front door. Mya never drove a motorized bike before, so it took her a few minutes to get right. Mya finally found out how to work the motorized part of the bike, and then she took off down the street. Mya looked at her watch and the timer that she had set, said that she had 12 minutes to make it to the abandoned warehouse. Mya looked to see if there was a faster speed on the bike and she found out that there was. Mya switched to the ultimate speed and then she started to feel hopeful that she would make it there in time.

"Yes!" Mya said as the bike sped down the Ave. On the way there, Mya started to think about what was going to happen. Mya knew that she could not afford to waste time by getting caught up in her overthinking, so Mya shook it off, refocused and decided that she was going to handle matters as they came.

Mya took one last look at her watch and noticed that she had 2 minutes left. When Mya got to the corner of Job and Calendar Street, she could see someone flashing a light from inside the abandoned warehouse. Mya threw the bike down in front of the building and ran inside as fast as she could. Mya got to the middle of the abandoned warehouse and yelled out,

"I'm here. What do I do next?" Someone slowly came from out of the dark, however, they were approaching Mya from behind.

"Don't turn around or there will be consequences. You will ask no questions, but you will silently stand there and listen to my voice.

Do I make myself clear?" the masked person asked. Mya shook her head yes.

"First off, I just want to let you know that your little so-called boyfriend is safe, for now. Secondly, you will tell no one and I do mean absolutely no one, about what is happening right now. Thirdly, I warn you to start paying attention to who you surround yourself with and keep in mind that everything ain't always what it seems. Fourthly, treat life from this day forward, as if you are in a never-ending game of Chess and Lastly, your little boyfriend will be let go soon, as long as you stay in line. One little misstep and I can't guarantee that you or any of the people you love, will be safe. Now walk out this warehouse and understand that under no circumstances, do you turn around."

Mya was breathing heavily as she sped walk out of the abandoned warehouse. When Mya got outside, she bent over and took a deep breath because she was relieved that she didn't lose her life. A million and one thoughts were racing through Mya's mind as she made her way back home.

CHAPTER 16

Mya thought about the masked person telling her that she is not to say anything to anyone. Mya then thought about Juelz telling someone. Mya was so deep in thought, that she didn't realize she had made it home already. Mya rode the bike to the back of the house and without thinking about it, she hit the open-door button on her keychain which was connected to the garage door. Mya knew that the automatic sensor was not working, however when she hit the open button, the garage door automatically lifted. Mya confusingly hopped off the bike and walked it into the garage.

"This shit is driving me the fuck crazy. What the hell is going on?" Mya asked herself. Mya parked the bike where she found it and walked inside the house. Just as Mya was going up the kitchen backstairs, she received a FaceTime call from Juelz.

"Oh my god! I'm so glad to hear from you. Are you ok babe?" she asked Juelz. "Yeah, I'm good," Juelz answered nonchalantly.

"Where are you?" Mya asked.

"I'm right down the street from your house on Pine," he answered.

"I'm on my way to you. I'll come in through your window again." Juelz continued. "Ok bae. See you when you get here," she said and then Juelz hung up the phone.

Mya ran upstairs and headed towards Genie's room to see if she was still asleep. Mya quietly opened Genie's door and she was snoring. Mya quietly closed the door and tiptoed back to her room. Mya plopped down on her bed and then she received a text message from an unknown number. The text read, 'remember what I told you. I have eyes and ears everywhere.' Mya tossed her phone on her bed as Juelz was softly tapping on her window.

Juelz crawled in through the window and Mya put her finger up to her mouth to signal to Juelz to be quiet. Juelz went over and locked her bedroom door and Mya softly yelled,

"No, don't lock it. Genie doesn't allow locked doors around here, plus she is going to know something is up". Juelz locked the door anyway and Mya knew that this was not the time to get into an argument with him. Juelz silently sat on the edge of Mya's bed. Mya moved closer to Juelz and put her arms around him. It took Juelz some time before he said a word. Without making eye contact with Mya, he said,

"What did whoever you met in the abandoned warehouse say to you?" Mya told Juelz what was said and then Mya asked Juelz,

"What else was done and said to you?" Juelz was nervously bouncing his leg up and down and he said,

"Nothing else was done to me and whoever this nigga was, somehow let me know that this shit was personal." Mya then asked,

"What makes you say that?"

Juelz kept bouncing his leg up and down and then answered,

"I could just feel it. Whoever this nigga is, also threatened my family, talmbout I better not tell nobody anything other than what was seen on the FaceTime call". Mya just sat there at a loss for words and then Juelz asked Mya,

"Aye yo. Do you have ANY idea who this person could be?" Mya immediately answered,

"No. Mya then went on to say, "I never had any type of smoke with anyone that would cause them to do some nutty ass shit like this." Juelz jumped up and started lowkey spazzing out and then he said,

"This shit is prolly your fuckin' fault yo. I hope this nigga that I got into it with at The Square, didn't have nothing to do with this shit! Mya honestly didn't know what sneaky link (1) was or was not capable of doing.

Mya continued to sit there speechless and they both did not know what to say to each other. Mya finally asked Juelz,

"So have you thought about your next move is going to be?" Juelz started to pace around the room and said,

"Nah, not forreal, but trust Imma handle this shit!" Juelz looked Mya dead in the eyes and said,

"You just make sure that you do your part and don't tell NOBODY about this shit yo. Our families lives are in jeopardy." Mya softly said, "trust me. You don't have to worry about me saying shit to no one." Juelz started walking over to the window and said to Mya, "imma holla at you later." Mya thought that Juelz was going to give her a kiss goodbye, but he just coldly walked off and made his way out of the window.

Mya walked over to her bedroom door and locked the window. Mya made her way over to her desk where her laptop was and opened up her Vlog. Mya blankly stared at the screen for about 10 minutes before she started recording.

"Hey there my fellow Myatians. I know that it has been a while since my last post, but what can I say? Teenager bullshit. Right?! Have you all missed me? Because I have truly missed hanging out with y'all. My purpose for today's Vlog is to talk about 'real life' and what that means to me. I also want to know what that means to y'all. For me, 'real life' is talking about and dealing with the issues of your day. It is so easy for us to go through traumatic shit throughout the day, and then hop on our socials' and create this type of fantasy world that we can temporarily escape to.

Rather it be issues with boys, which seems to be the root of all of our problems, cyber bullies, or just waking up, there is always something that happens and it can either make or break our entire day. What I am going to share with you today, is my real life situation and it deals with making choices. As teenagers, how are we to know which choice is best to make? I mean, besides what our family, friends and associates tell us, how do we REALLY know what the right choices are? I mean really. Is there really a definition of what a good choice is and what a bad choice is? On top of all the drama that comes with our teenage lives, we are faced with making decisions. If you're an over-thinker like me, when faced with having to make a choice, it opens up a whole new world of infinite questions. Like, how will this choice affect me? Affect my family? Will I create another problem if I make this choice? I see that my comments are blowing up with what you guys think, so I am going to choose some lucky Myatian to go live with."

Mya started to scroll up through some of the previous comments that were made while she was talking. Mya then scrolled back down to her incoming comments and she received a DM that read, "DON'T DO IT!! Mya froze in front of the camera and the comments from her Myatians were coming through telling her that her screen had frozen. Mya snapped out of it and quickly said,

"Oh my god! I am so sorry Myatians. I am having some technical issues, but I promise you I will be back ASAP." Mya threw up a peace sign and blew kisses at her followers as she said,

"Until next time my fellow Myatians. Be great!" Mya immediately closed her laptop and jumped up to go to her bathroom to throw some water on her face.

Mya splashed some cold water on her face and just stared at herself in the mirror and said, "come on Mya.

You have to pull your shit together and figure this shit out." Mya dried her face and walked over to her bed and grabbed the phone. Mya laid across her bed on her back and she FaceTimed her dad.

"Heeeyyy baby girl. I was beginning to think you were mad at me," Mya's dad cheerfully answered. "No daddy, I am not mad at you. It's just teenage stuff, you know?" "Yeah baby girl. I definitely understand. So what's on your mind?" Mya's dad asked.

Mya took a deep sigh before she answered and she said,

"Did mamma call you and tell you about tomorrow? He answered,

"Yes she did baby girl, but I won't be able to take you because this is my weekend to be on call and they called me in to cover for someone tomorrow morning." Mya sucked her teeth and asked,

"Then how am I supposed to get there because you already know that Genie ain't going to drive no hour and ½." Mya's dad paused and took a deep breath and said,

"I know that you are not going to like this, but Geraldine is going to take you and then pick you up." Geraldine was Mya's dad's new wife and absolutely no one liked her except the younger twins. Geraldine and Mya's dad had 2 boys and 1 girl that were younger than the twins. Mya sucked her teeth and said,

"See daddy this is why I was calling to tell you, that I really really need my own car."

CHAPTER 17

Geraldine was an ER surgeon, and she was the breadwinner in the marriage. However, Mya's dad was a number guy, and he made plenty of bread himself. Mya's dad paused and then said to Mya, "baby girl. You know that we have talked about this. Genie, your mom and I don't think that you are responsible enough to have your own car."

Mya started to whine, "But Daddy, that is not fair! I am a straight-A student, and I don't get into any trouble!"

"Yes, I am very proud of you for that, but Mya, you know about the issues that we have dealt with in the past, with you and your underage drinking."

Mya remained silent, and she started crying. "I understand that, but Daddy, this isn't fair. All the Warriors have their own cars, and I haven't had any issues with my drinking in the past two years."

Mya's dad hesitated and said, "Yes, this is true; however, you know I still have to discuss this with your mamma, Genie, and Geraldine."

"I understand," Mya softly answered.

Mya's dad was definitely sweet on all of his girls and Mya played on this. As Mya sat on the FaceTime call with her sad puppy dog eyes, her dad said,

"OK, baby girl. I will talk to Geraldine this evening, and then tomorrow, I'll talk to Genie, and when you go to visit your mamma, tell her I said call me so that she and I can talk about this."

Mya's mood immediately changed as she answered while kicking her legs in excitement, "ok. Thank you, daddy. I really appreciate you," then Mya kissed her phone.

"Alright, baby girl. I gotta go attend to your brothers and sisters, and we'll finish this discussion later. Ok?"

"OKAY, daddy. Love you!" Mya said as she disconnected from the conversation.

Mya laid on the bed, happy as hell, and then her mood suddenly changed because she thought about all the bullshit that was going on in her life. Mya lay on her bed in a daze and then she started talking to Mykel out loud.

"Okay, big bro. I need your help. What the fuck am I supposed to do now? I can't tell anybody what is going on with me and I don't know how to feel."

As Mya was talking to her dead brother, out loud, she slowly drifted off into a deep sleep and started to dream. Mya had a dream that she and the Warriors were walking home from school and they spotted the black Chevy. The Warriors started to haul ass towards an unknown house and they busted the window out so that they could get in. As the Warriors made it through the window, there was a person dressed in all black who was standing in the corner of the room, with his face in the wall.

The Warriors all started screaming and then the person who was standing there said, "I mean you no harm, but you girls are in great danger."

Ktru started walking towards the person and the person yelled out for her to stop, as if they had eyes in the back of their head.

Ktru immediately stopped in her tracks and Asia yelled out, "Who are you? And what do you want from us?"

The person in the corner did not answer, however, a film started playing on the wall. The Warriors were confused as they silently watched the video that was playing on the wall. The video was a flashback of when the Warriors made their very first friendship pact in kindergarten. The video showed Mya playing in the sandbox with some classmates that Mya did not remember, it then went on to show how Rainah was swinging on the swings, Asia was going down the slide and Sklyer was with a group of white girls. The white girls that Skyler was with, started to make fun of her clothes, and the group of girls were shown teasing Skyler and then throwing a ball at her head. Skyler started crying, ran over to a tree, and hid behind it.

Mya was shown throwing her sand bucket to the side and running over to the group of girls who were bullying Skyler.

Standing alone, Mya approached the group of girls and said, "Why don't y'all pick on somebody your own size?"

The group of girls started laughing and the leader of the pact started pushing Mya around. "What are you going to do about it? There are 4 of us and only 1 of you".

The group of girls started pushing Mya around and then all the kids on the playground started screaming, "Fight! Fight! Fight! As they ran over to be onlookers of the drama. Ktru, Rainah, and Asia all ran over to the crowd, saw that the group of girls were pushing Mya around and then they all started swinging on the group of girls.

The adults on the playground were already on their way over to the crowd. The teachers could be seen yelling, "Alright everyone. Back it up!"

As they were breaking up the fight between the girls that came to save Mya, the teachers separated the girls and told Mya, Rainah, Ktru, and Asia to go stand over by the tree where Skyler was hiding behind. They all gathered around Skyler and asked if she was ok.

Skyler shook her head and said, "Yes."

While the teachers were busy getting all their classmates back in order, Mya said to Rainah, Ktru, and Asia, "Hi, my name is Mya. What are your names?"

They all introduced themselves and then Mya said, "Thank you all for having my back."

The girls all replied, "You're welcome."

Mya said, "We have to stick together."

Then she stuck out her pinky finger and asked, "Best friends forever?"

All the girls, including Skyler, grabbed each other's pinkies and said, "Best friends forever!"

The funny thing was that Mya's dream was actually the true story behind how the Warriors first met. Mya's dream was suddenly interrupted by Genie coming into her room and telling her that dinner was on the stove.

Mya sat up in her bed and said, "Thank you Genie. I will be down in a second."

Mya sat on her bed, replaying the dream she had, and then once again she started talking to Mykel out loud. "Ok, big bro. What did that dream mean? It's a true story, but how does that relate to what is going on now?”

Mya jumped up out of her bed and headed downstairs to get dinner. Genie was in the kitchen, making Mya's plate and putting the rest of the food in Tupperware. Genie looked at Mya and could tell that something was wrong with her.

Genie said to Mya, “Are you okay chile? You've really been actin' strange for the past few days and I'm worried bout you.”

Mya grabbed her plate and headed over to sit at the kitchen table. Genie stopped putting the food away, went over to the kitchen table, and sat with Mya.

Genie sat down, grabbed both of Mya's hands and said, “Look at me chile. Mya turned to look Genie in her eyes and Genie said, “Can't nobody help you if you don't let somebody know what they need to do in order to help?”

Mya just burst into tears and Genie just sat there, still holding her hands and waiting for Mya to respond.

Mya finally said, “Genie, do you remember what your life was like when you were my age?” Genie sucked her teeth and said, “Whew chile. I know it's been quite some time ago, but I still remember it like it was yesterday. Mya didn't say anything so Genie kept talking. Chile, since you ain't talkin', all I'm going to say to you is this, “Experience is the greatest teacher and no matter how fine of a job that we have all done with raising you, when you leave outta this house, the choice is yours and yours alone."

Genie got up from the table, gave Mya a big hug, and then kissed her on the forehead and said, "no matter what you do and what choice you make, your family will always choose you."

Mya took a minute before she said, "Thank you Genie. I love you so much."

Genie answered, "I know darling. And I will always love you in life and in death."

Mya started eating the fried chicken, corn on the cob, and baked macaroni that Genie had fixed. Genie was born in the south and she came from a long generation of religious folk. Although Mya didn't really claim a certain religion the only thing that she was raised around, was Christianity. Genie could sense that her grandbaby was still crying so she started singing her favorite song by Rev. Paul Jones. "I've had some good days. I've had some hills to climb. I have some weary days. And some sleepless nights. But when I look around. And think things over. All of my good days. Outweigh my bad days and I-I, I won't complain." Mya could no longer keep inside the deep cry that she had been trying to get out ever since this drama started. Genie stopped singing and said, "That's alright chile. Let it all out. Crying is good for the soul."

Genie put all the food in the refrigerator then walked over to Mya, gently patted her on the shoulder, and said, "You gone be alright baby. You will figure it out. You always do. That's the stock you come from and the DNA that runs through your veins, chile. You are a Warrior."

Genie walked off into the living room and Mya received a FaceTime call from the Warriors. Mya had already lost her appetite because she could not stop crying, so when the Warriors called her, she put her plate of food in the microwave and headed up the kitchen stairs.

Mya wiped her tears away and pulled herself together and then she answered, "Hey bitches! Is everyone cool?"

All the girls started saying "yes" as Mya entered her bedroom and then shut the door.

Skyler started by saying, "bitch. I saw you made a post on your Vlog earlier! Why did you end it all sus style?"

Mya quickly responded and said, "Girl, I heard Genie coming down the hallway and I knew that she was coming straight to my room."

The Warriors all started laughing and then Asia said, "Well I am sure that you either heard from Juelz or he was over there. Yao told me that he was on the bricks."

"yea. He was here," Mya nonchalantly said.

Rainah then said, "Well, did he tell you anything about who kidnapped him? Because he didn't tell the Brothers shit!"

Mya looked straight into her call and said, "Girl, that nigga didn't tell me shit. The only thing he did when he came over here was accuse me of being the reason that shit happened to him."

CHAPTER 18

Ktru said, "I figured his nutty ass would think some bullshit like that."

Mya felt something come over her that made her want to share what she had dreamed about. Instead of telling the Warriors about the dream, Mya said, "y'all know what I have been thinking about since all this shit popped off?"

"Do tell," Skyler said.

"Remember that time in kindergarten when we were on the playground?"

The Warriors all became hype and started saying, "hell yea bitch!" They all started laughing as each of them started to share what they remembered about that day.

Skyler started off by saying, "Bitch! How could I ever forget? You bitches came ridin' for me!"

Asia said, "hell yeah bitch. I remember when I pulled that one bitch by the hair and slammed her to the ground!"

Rainah added, "Yessss. Then remember when fat-ass Ms. Fletcher came through the crowd. Knocking little kids over like a fat, mad-ass bull?"

Skyler then said, "What I remember the most is the pinky pact that we all made."

The Warriors all yelled out together, "Best friends forever!"

Mya seemed to be an emotional wreck these days and she started crying. The girls saw how hurt their friend was and then suddenly, they all started crying.

"I fuckin' love you bitches!" Mya said between tears.

Asia started laughing while she was crying and said, "bitch we fuckin love you more."

Ktru then said, "bitch you already know, that we are here for you. Maybe not from the cradle, but most definitely to the grave bitch!"

The Warriors all started saying, "Yessss bitch."

Mya suddenly remembered why they had and always could trust one another. Their friendship and sisterhood had been tried and tested so many times and at the end of each test, they came out on top, together, solid as a rock.

Rainah then said, "I speak for all of us when I say this friend. There ain't nothin' in this world that we wouldn't do for you. We been through too much shit, for our loyalty to be questioned, by ANYONE, for a fuckin' second."

Mya started wiping tears from her eyes, then she received an incoming call from Sneaky Link (1).

Mya ignored the call, but she did tell the Warriors that she would call them back. "Imma call y'all right back real quick. I gotta handle something real fast," she said to them. "Ok den," Skyler answered.

"Make sure you call us right back bitch, "Asia added.

"We know that there is something that you have to tell us," Rainah added.

"I got y'all," Mya said and they hung up. Mya took a few minutes to think about what she wanted to say to Sneaky Link 1, and also thought about what he needed to say to her." Mya fixed her hair, made sure all tears were wiped from her face and then she FaceTimed Sneaky Link 1.

"What's the deal, trouble?" He said to Mya.

"Ain't shit. What's going on wit you?" she asked.

"I was thinking about you, plus I saw the Vlog that you just posted and it looked like something was up with you. Everything cool?" He asked.

Without hesitation, Mya let him know that there was nothing to worry about.

"Is that all you wanted my nigga?" Mya asked him.

"Damn yo'. It's like that? What the fuck did I do to you?" He asked.

Mya huffed and sucked her teeth, and she said, "I just don't want to be bothered Period." "Imma let your moody ass go, but before I hang up yo, just remember that you caused this Muthafuckin smoke."

Mya wanted to start tweaking on this nigga, but she knew that she had to play it smart because she needed to get as much info from him as possible.

"What the fuck are you talmbout?" Mya asked.

"Exactly what the fuck I said, yo. You the fuckin' reason why that bitch ass nigga snuck me!"

"So what the fuck is you really trynna say, my nigga?" Mya yelled.

Sneaky Link looked deep into Mya's face and said to her, "What I'm not bout to do is go back and forth with you, Mya. I neva had beef wit this nigga, and I neva will beef wit a nigga," and then he hung up.

Mya sat there staring into space as she was trying to figure out what this nigga was trying to say. Mya started talking to herself, "I wonder if he had something to do with kidnapping Juelz? Is he the nigga that keeps following us the fuck around in the city, in that Chevy?" Mya switched gears because she really wanted to call the Warriors back and let them know what was going on. Mya FaceTimed the Warriors and they were all happy to hear from her.

"I'm glad you actually called us right back bitch," Ktru said.

Mya stuck her middle finger up and said, "Okay bitches, here's the deal. First off, I didn't tell y'all that I might be pregnant. The Warriors all gave shocked reactions, even Asia. Mya noticed that Asia did not react and Mya knew that she didn't want the Warriors to know that she already knew. Mya then went on to say, this is the most embarrassing, but I have been drinking early in the morning before school again."

The Warriors gave different reactions, but none of them said anything; they just listened. Mya ended by saying, the most embarrassing thing that I ever had to tell y'all, is that I have been doing coke ever since Mykel's murder".

The Warriors sat on the FaceTime call silently as they looked at one another. No one really had a clue whether to react or not, so Mya chose to break the silence.

"I know all you bitches either have something to say or tons of questions. Go ahead and give it to me," she said.

The silence continued for about two minutes, and then Rainah started off by saying, "First off bitch. Personally, I want to let you know that I am super proud of you for being brave enough to share those things with us."

Skyler then said, "bitch you already know that we all have our secrets, and ain't nobody judging you."

Ktru chimed in and said, "That's right, bestie. We are happy that you felt comfortable enough to share these things with us, and now you don't have to go through this shit alone."

"I know that's right," Asia added. Asia then went on to say, to show you how much I appreciate your bravery and to let you know that we, in fact, all do have our secrets, I wanna take this time to share with y'all that my parents' nail and spa salon, give "Happy endings" to certain, trusted customers."

All the Warriors grabbed their faces in shock, and then they all started laughing.

Rainah started with her moment of truth and said, "Well, since we are in the sharing secrets mode, I sell narcotics illegally."

The Warriors all laughed again and then Skyler shared. "Well, I'm adopted. I found out when I was 10 years old."

Ktru then said, "Well, I guess that leaves me huh? I had an abortion last year and Jihad does not know about it."

The Warriors all looked around at one another and they could feel the connection between them, becoming stronger than ever.

Mya then said, "Oh, I forgot to add that I have someone that I have in my contacts as sneaky link #1 and his name is Dylan."

Ktru already knew about the sneaky link, but the rest of the Warriors didn't. Mya then told the Warriors that Dylan was 20 years old and was a first-year student at Better University, which was a community college.

"To be honest y'all, although I might be pregnant, I haven't told Juelz. Juelz also didn't know about Dylan before that shit popped off at the Square last night, but I am damn sure that he is either sus or for sure, about my situation-ship with Dylan."

"Damn bitches, I need to smoke," Rainah said as she rolled a wood.

Skyler then lightened the mood by singing, "O O O, O'Reilly!"

The Warriors all laughed. The Warriors continued on FaceTime, talking about random things and then Mya received a text message with a SnapChat friend invite and the message read, "Check this story ASAP". Mya was still not comfortable with sharing her secret about her sneaky link (2), however, Mya did feel comfortable enough to tell the Warriors that she had just received a Snap friend link to view a story.

Mya took a minute and thought about it before she told the Warriors because she wasn't sure. Mya then remembered that each time the unknown caller contacted her, they always told Mya what she should not do. This time whoever PeekABoo was, did not say anything like this, in their message.

Mya then went on to say, "bitch! I just got a Snap message from user PeekABoo and I don't know who da fuck this is."

Asia said, "Accept the invite bitch and then share your screen with us."

Mya accepted the invite to view the story and then shared her screen with the Warriors. The story starts with the inside of a hospital and then it shows a baby nursery. The story then showed a family picture of Mya and all of her siblings, when their parents first married. The last picture was a graveyard and then it ended.

"What the fuck was that?" Rainah yelled.

Asia said to Mya, "Girl, go and click on PeekABoo's profile right now."

Mya was still sharing her screen when she went back to the same invite link, but an error message appeared. Skyler's dad was this high-profile tech guy. He was so dope that he spent 5 years in jail for hacking a company's stock profile.

Skyler said, "That error message means that the user never existed. I'm going to ask my dad about it and let y'all know what he comes back with."

"Good looking," Mya said.

Ktru said, "What do you think that shit means, Mya?"

Mya stared into space and said, "Off top, I have no fuckin' clue!"

Rainah said, "Are you going to tell anyone about this?"

Mya looked around her room and said, "I honestly don't know. I have to sleep on this shit." "Damn Gina! This whole situation is nutty as fuck," Skyler said.

"Fuck yea!" Mya added.

Asia then said, "So Mya, just think about all the shit that has popped off since yesterday until now. If you had to take your best guess, what do you think all this could mean?"

Mya stared off into space for about 1 minute before she answered and said, "That is the shit that is fuckin' me up. I really don't fuckin' know!" Mya suddenly remembered that she was going to see her mamma tomorrow, so she said to the Warriors, "I am supposed to go see my mamma tomorrow morning. I definitely am going to run all this shit by her and see what she thinks."

"That sounds like the move," Ktru said.

The Warriors all sat on the FaceTime call, silent. During the time they were silent, Rainah was hitting her wood, Mya was sipping on her drink, Ktru was texting Jihad, Skyler was sitting looking at everyone like they were crazy, and Asia could be seen trying to piece all the shit together.

CHAPTER 19

Damn bitches! What are we going to do?" Asia asked.

In this moment, Mya knew that she needed to get away somewhere where she could actually have some peace and quiet and then try to figure this all out. Some years back, the Warriors discovered The Secret Path together. However, neither of them has been back there for years, let alone by themselves. Mya let the Warriors know that she was headed there. Ktru said, "Mya you know I would go with you friend, but Jihad was real serious about me sittin' still until he finds out what's going on."

Skyler then said, "Yeah, unfortunately, friend, I am in the same boat with Ktru."

Mya was looking at them as if she didn't know what they were talking about.

"What bitch?" Ktru asked.

Mya sucked her teeth and then said, "I don't remember invitin' either of ya'll bitches!"

Asia clapped her hands and was like, "Yess, bitch. That part!"

The Warriors started laughing.

Rainah added, "All jokes aside, bestie, please, please, please keep your head on a swivel and at least Snap us when you get there AND when you make it back home!"

"I got you," Mya said.

Mya started to blowing the Warriors kisses and then Skyler said, "Plus bitch. Let us know if anything happens or you hear anything. You already know that we got you."

"You already!" Mya replied.

The Warriors were all blowing kisses at one another and saying their goodbyes as they ended the FaceTime chat. Mya wanted to be comfortable going there, so she decided to change into some sweats, a hoodie with no shirt underneath, socks, and slides.

Mya made sure that she had her phone and air pods and then she headed towards Genie's room to let her know where she was leaving. Genie already knew about The Secret Path, so Mya was relieved that she didn't have to pull a juke move. Mya knocked on the door and it was as if Genie was sitting in her makeup chair, waiting for her. "Come on in chile," Genie said to Mya before she could even knock on the door. Mya slowly opened the door because she was not sure what she was going to have to deal with when she opened it. Genie told Mya to go and have a seat on the lounge chair that sat in front of her dresser. Mya sat and the chair and started to spin around in the chair, like a little excited kid who was about to receive a present.

Mya spun back around in the chair and faced the mirror and then Genie walked up behind her, placed her hands on each side of Mya's shoulder, and said, "My, my, my! Look at you chile. You are just as beautiful as you want to be!" Mya looked at Genie with confusion because she wasn't sure what was going on.

"Everything ok Genie?" she asked as she stared at Genie through the mirror.

"Yes, chile. Everything is fine. It's just that yesterday was your Seventeenth birthday and I realized, I never told my grandbaby how beautiful of a young woman you have grown to be. I am proud of you Mya. We all are proud of you."

Mya reached one of her hands up so that he laid on top of Genie's hand and replied, "Thank you Genie. I really appreciate it and needed to hear that right now."

Genie reached into her house robe pocket and pulled out an ankle bracelet. Genie sat on the edge of her bed and told Mya to spin around in the chair and put her leg into her lap so that she could place the bracelet on Mya's ankle. Mya pulled her socks off, pulled up her sweatpants legs, and was smiling from ear to ear as she turned to place her right leg on Genie's lap. Genie softly patted Mya's foot and started to put the ankle bracelet on. Genie said absolutely nothing, as she put the anklet on. The anklet had diamond studded, small hearts, all around it. As Genie placed the anklet on, it clung to Mya's body as if it was specially made for her. Mya jumped up and ran over to Genie's full-body mirror that hung on her closet door and started to spin around and admire the jewelry that was lightly pinging off the lights.

"OMG Genie. Thank you sooooooo much!" Mya yelped as she went over to give Genie a big hug.

Genie kissed Mya on her forehead and said, "Happy Birthday baby. Now go and git outta here!" Genie said with a slight giggle.

Mya ran over to the chair where she had taken off her slides and socks, grabbed them up, and as she was running out of the room she said, "Thanks again Genie. I'll be back. Headed to The Secret Path!" and then she slammed the door in excitement. Mya started pulling down her pant legs, putting on her socks as she headed down the stairs. Mya couldn't quite understand why she felt so excited about receiving this bracelet from Genie, because she was no stranger to getting jewels. Mya brushed it off and slowly opened up the front door to peep out the scenery.

The coast was clear, and Mya headed out the front door, still being sure that she stayed on point. Mya decided that she wasn't going to put her earbuds in because she wanted to make sure she was ready. Mya quickly headed to the back of the house as she was still looking up and down her street. Mya jogged towards Vanderbilt Drive and knew that once she got behind a certain row of houses, she could relax. Mya stopped jogging once she made it to safety, however she still didn't put her earbuds in. Mya looked at her Apple watch to check the time, it was 5:55 pm. Mya made her way to the bushes and started to push the trees and leaves to the side. Mya finally arrived at the beginning of The Secret Path which led to an entire world that seemed only known to a select few people in Atlanta.

On this Secret Path, there were big, beautiful trees, streams of fresh river water streams, fish that she had never seen before, dirt paths, beautiful flower patches, and big boulders that were spread out along the streams. There was a particular place where The Warriors all would hang out whenever they visited there years ago. Mya made her way to that place. Mya found their spot, kicked off her slides and socks, and went to sit on the small boulder by the stream that allowed her to put her feet into the water. Mya placed her air pods in her ears and began to think back to everything that had happened since Friday morning. As Mya sat there, kicking her feet back and forth in the water, she felt a pair of hands gently touch her shoulders. The touch was so soft, warming, and gentle, that Mya didn't even turn around to see who or what it was. Whoever was behind Mya, spoke very low, but softly, and Mya could barely hear their voice.

The voice whispered, "Close your eyes and let me take you somewhere."

Mya relaxed, closed her eyes, and allowed her thoughts to take over, immediately she thought back to the time when her younger twin brother and sister were born. Mya was six years old when the twins were born and, in this memory, it was Mya, the older triplets, daddy, mamma, Genie, and Nana at the hospital. Nana was Genie's mom, but Mya hadn't seen her since Mya was 10 years old. Nana was placed in an old folks home back home in Tennessee, shortly after the twins were born. Nana struggled with mental health problems, but Alzheimer's is what made her health go down super fast. So much so, that it was too much for Mamma and Daddy to handle, on top of Mya and her Brothers and sisters. Genie could not care for her because she was taking care of Pop-Pop with his cancer.

Mya always felt as though she was Nana's favorite because Mya was the only one that Nana had a nickname for. Nana always called Mya, "My Angel."

Mamma and Daddy told Mya that is where her name came from. In this memory Mya was having, during the twin's birth, Mya remembered that she went to go out in the waiting room to sit with Nana. Everyone else was in the delivery room with Mamma and Daddy. Mya remembered sitting next to Nana and Mya sat beside her, hugged her from the side, and laid her head on Nana's shoulder. Nana didn't say anything, she just placed her hand on top of Mya's, started humming some unknown old negro spiritual and rocking from side to side. Mya didn't even know why, but Mya just started crying. Mya remembered that Nana's humming just became louder as Mya silently cried her eyes out.

In the memory, Mya remembered that Nana started to wipe Mya's tears and patted her lap, signaling Mya to come and sit on her lap. Mya jumped out of her chair and jumped into Nana's lap.

Mya remembered softly grabbing Nana's hand and she looked deep into her eyes and said to her, "I want you to always remember something, My Angel. No matter how near or how far, I will always be with you, but most importantly I want you to remember that You are My Angel." Nana kissed Mya on the forehead and that was the last time conversation Mya remembers having with Nana because she had gotten really sick after that.

Mya's memory was suddenly interrupted by a call that blared through her earphones. Mya's body jumped as she shook her head and she noticed that it was starting to get dark. Mya turned around quickly to see who was there with her and there was no one there.

CHAPTER 20

Mya looked down at her watch to see who was calling, and it was Juelz. Mya wasn't sure if she wanted to deal with whatever smoke he did or didn't have.

Mya took a long breath and answered, "What's up?" Mya didn't put Juelz on FaceTime, and he felt some kinda way.

"Why you didn't pick up the video chat?" Juelz asked.

Mya continued to put on her socks and slid back on as she ignored his question. Juelz got dead silent and Mya knew that he was ear hustlin' trying to listen for background noises. Mya finished putting her stuff back on and continued walking down the path to leave. Mya waited until she made it to a nearby wooded area and then accepted his FaceTime call.

"Mya continued to walk without looking into the camera and said, "Happy now?" Mya side-eyed Juelz and could see that he was putting in major energy, trying to figure out where she was.

"What's wrong with you?" Juelz asked Mya because he could see that she had dried tears on her cheek.

"Same ole shit Juelz. The story of my fucking life!" Mya answered.

Juelz sucked his teeth and said, "I believe you mean the story of OUR fucking lives!"

Mya shook her head and just kept walking.

Anyway, yo. "Where the fuck you at? I thought I told your hard-headed ass not to leave the crib until you heard from me?" he asked Mya.

"Look nigga. I appreciate you trying to look out and protect a bitch and all that, but you not my fuckin' daddy!"

Mya then turned to face Juelz and he was smoking a wood. Juelz blew the smoke into the phone and said, "Yeah, you right," and then he hung up.

Mya didn't even have the desire or energy to go back and forth with him, so she didn't even bother to call him back. Mya just FaceTimed the Warriors instead.

They all answered, "What's up bitch!"

Mya turned her phone and twirled all around so that the Warriors could get a view of The Secret Path.

Asia made the first comment/joke, "Yesss, Daniel Sun, we need to go visit there soon!"

The Warriors laughed and then Skyler said, "when was the last time that we were actually all there?"

Rainah immediately answered, "2 years ago on the day that I was diagnosed with Leukemia." The Warriors were all silent for about two minutes before Ktru said, "damn bitch! Leave it up to yo ass to fuck up a wet dream!" The Warriors started laughing and Mya let the Warriors know that she had to hang up because she was leaving the Secret Path and she needed to concentrate on watching her back and getting to the crib safely.

Mya headed towards the Ave and per usual, she started over thinking shit. Mya started a conversation in her head. "This shit is bananas. It's like I'm in a never-ending nightmare. Whoever this person or persons is, why must they taunt? Why don't they just do what the fuck they gotta do and keep that shit pushing?!"

Suddenly, someone came up from behind Mya, threw a cloth bag over her head, and tossed her into a vehicle. The vehicle sped about 2 blocks away and then it stopped in its tracks. Mya's body tumbled towards the front of the vehicle, and then she heard someone getting close to her. Mya started kicking and screaming and then she noticed that her feet, hands, and the cloth bag, were not tied.

Mya angrily snatched the bag off of her head and Juelz was staring Mya dead in the face.

Mya started smacking Juelz's body, pushing him back and saying, "Why the fuck you do this nutty shit bro? You ain't throwing no type of rizz on our situation with this bullshit."

Juelz thought the shit was funny as hell because he could not stop laughing. Between laughs, Juelz said to Mya, "That's what ya dumb ass git! I told you to sit your stupid ass still until you get word. You don't fuckin' listen!" Mya was so angry that she couldn't even respond, instead she just kept shaking her head and rocking back and forth in anger.

Juelz looked at Mya like she had 8 heads and said, "You buggin' yo. It ain't even that serious. I just wanted to show you how easily you could be touched." Mya blankly stared at Juelz and then he saw that Mya wasn't going to switch her attitude. He sucked his teeth, jumped in the front seat of the van, and called his Brothers.

"Yizzo," Jihad answered.

The rest of the Brothers chimed in with their greetings and then Juelz said, "We still going to the River?" The River was a drive-in movie theater. There was also a huge piece of grassy area where people could put down their blankets and chairs, to watch the movie.

"You already," Rock said. We can all meet up at my spot and the Warriors can ride in Juelz's pops van and we can slide in my ride," Rock continued.

"Sounds like a plan," Yao said.

"Alright then yo. Be there in 10," Juelz said.

Juelz ended the call and jumped in the back of the van and went to sit down beside Mya and then he hugged her.

"What's on your mind baby?" he asked Mya.

Mya looked at Juelz and said, "How do you know if I'm even in the mood to go to the river? You ordering my steps now?"

Juelz looked at Mya for about a minute and then said, "You done?" Mya shrugged her shoulders. Juelz knew that in order to change Mya's attitude, he had to kiss her ass so he said, "Babe, you forgive me for doing this nutty ass shit to you? could you show me forgiveness by coming with me to the River?"

Juelz looked at Mya with puppy dog eyes while acting like he was whimpering. Mya looked at Juelz and said, "I don't like this type of begging. It's not a good look on you." Juelz and Mya started laughing and then Juelz started kissing Mya on her neck.

Mya was trying to fight him off because she was still upset about the shit he just pulled, but Juelz knew that when he kissed Mya's body, she became like putty in his hands. Mya gave in and became putty in his hands. Juelz started sucking on Mya's nipples, through her hoodie. While he sucked on her nipples, he reached inside Mya's sweatpants and started pussy popping her. Mya became so turned on, that she sucked hard on Juelz's neck, leaving a big ass hickey. The moans of Juelz and Mya filled the van. Juelz sat on the small seat that was in the back and slapped his lap and Mya knew that this was code for, "Come sit on this dick."

Mya seductively crawled over to Juelz and then she slowly started taking off her hoodie. Mya slid the hoodie off over her head, cupped both of her titties, and started licking and sucking on her nipples.

Juelz was still in the seat, his dick was solid as a rock, and he started stroking his meat while he watched Mya strip and dance for him. Mya started swaying her body back and forth, as she listened to music in her mind. Mya took off her bra and threw it at Juelz. Then she turned around, bent over, and started seductively taking off her sweats.

"Bring all that big pretty ass to big dad," he said to Mya. Mya slowly walked backward, ass first towards Juelz.

He bit her on the ass and then slowly stuck his thumb in her ass. Mya's pussy started gushing and Juelz said, "yea. That's what I'm talmbout. Give me that ewwwe goowie."

Mya slowly sat on the tip of Juelz's dick, tightened her pussy walls, and rotated on his dick. Juelz screamed out in ecstasy.

Mya started slowly stroking his dick by going up and down, while she tightened her pussy walls. Mya spun around, roughly kissed

Juelz in the mouth, and said, "I have something to tell you, big dad."

Juelz was on the edge of bussin' a nut and he looked at Mya and said, "Babe, please don't fuck this moment up."

Mya didn't want to ruin it either, because Juelz had never felt so good while inside of her. Mya continued to ride the shit out of his dick and right before he was about to cum, Mya jumped off his dick, tapped him on his outer thigh, and said, "Come on bro. We gotta go meet up with the rest of the gang."

Juelz threw his head back into his hands and yelled, "You have got to be fuckin' kiddin' me yo! What the fuck are you doing??!!"

While Mya was putting her clothes back on, she smiled, looked at Juelz, and said, "You did that nutty ass shit to me on my birthday, I told you to remember that nigga!"

Juelz shook his head and started angrily starting buttoning his pants. "You right," Juelz said to Mya.

Mya started feeling some type of way and then she said, "hol up nigga. I know you ain't trippin'! Oh, so it's ok for you to do that shit to me, but it ain't no fun when the rabbit got the gun, is it?" Juelz looked at Mya and started putting his clothes back on in silence. Once Juelz had on all his clothes, he jumped in the driver's seat, still not saying anything to Mya. Mya jumped into the passenger seat, looked at Juelz, and said, "So, is this how the rest of the night is going to go? If so, you can just let me out right now and I can walk back to the crib".

Juelz looked at Mya and his look was so cold that Mya knew this nigga was saying without saying, "bitch, get out this van, and you gon see what it is."

Mya put on her seatbelt and didn't say anything to Juelz the entire ride to Rock's crib. Juelz couldn't handle the silence, so he said, "When we were fucking, you said that you had something to tell me. I didn't mean to cut you off, babe. It's just that ya timing was all fucked up! I'm all ears now, so tell me, what's on your mind?" Mya stared blankly out of the windshield and didn't answer anything Juelz was asking her. "So, this is what you gone to do the whole night yo?" he asked her. Mya still didn't answer him, so he stopped the van and told Mya to get out. "Yo. If this is what the rest of the night is going to be like, just go ahead and git the fuck out!" Juelz yelled. Mya didn't move a muscle. She turned and looked at Juelz like he was crazy, and he yelled and punched the steering wheel. "You get on my fuckin' nerves!!" and he sped off.

Juelz and Mya finally were pulling up to Rock's crib and the rest of the gang could be seen all standing outside. Juelz looked at Mya and said, "aye yo! Look at me."

Mya slowly turned her head to face Juelz and he said, "Mya cut the bullshit alright? We gone go watch this movie at the River, have a good time, and put all this petty shit to the side. Cool?"

Mya looked at Juelz and in a very low, whisper voice, she answered, "Ok Juelz." They both hopped out of the van and the Warriors all ran up to Mya and started hugging and kissing her.

"Ewwww! I smell pussy juice," Rainah jokingly said to Mya.

The Warriors started laughing and tickling Mya and then Mya yanked away from them, started laughing, and said, "Whateva bitch!" The Warriors all fell to the ground, kicking and laughing because they were high as fuck.

Yao came over to the Warriors and said, "Alright, alright, alright y'all cacklin' biddies. It's time to roll."

Asia threw her water bottle at Yao and said, "Whateva nigga! Don't be mad at us because we ain't in our feelings!"

CHAPTER 21

Everyone was doing their own thing as the Brothers all hopped in their SUV. Juelz came over to the Warriors and told Rainah to drive his jalopy van. Mya knew that this was another one of Juelz's pop shots, so Mya chose to not even respond. Juelz finally made a quick second of eye contact with Mya then he licked his lips as he tossed Rainah the keys. Rainah already peeped what had just happened and she yelled out to Juelz, as he was headed to the SUV, "Nigga I saw what you just did. Don't be trynna put me in y'all bullshit.! You know I don't even play wit my girl like that!" Julez waved Rainah off as he jumped in the back seat of the SUV.

As Mya was seated in the passenger side of the ride, Rainah looked over at her and asked, "Are you ok with this sis?"

Mya looked at Rainah and said, "Girl! You already know that this shit is a small thing to a giant!"

Rainah and all the Warriors replied, "I know that's right!"

Skyler then said to Mya, "Girl! Whateva you puttin' on that nigga Juelz, got him straight in nutty mode!"

Ktru said, "Bitch! I already told you that this shit is cute at first, but it will git really ugly if it goes unchecked!" Mya did not respond because she knew that the type of relationship that she and Juelz had, none of them would be able to understand how familiar they were with each other and their vibes.

Mya became agitated and yelled, "I said I'm good bitches, dam. Ain't nothin' to worry about!"

The Warriors all looked at one another, said nothing, and they let it go. "On our way to the River bitches! To watch this fuckin' scary jawn!" Ktru screamed. The Warriors all started laughing and then Rainah pulled out her pen and started passing it around.

"Come on bitches! We got to git litty so that we can entertain these kitties!" Rainah yelled.

The Warriors went crazy with laughter and there was nothing but good times and good vibes. The gang all pulled up to The River at the same time and everyone hopped out of their rides.

"So, I guess we over in the grass this evening?" Skyler asked.

"Looks like it", Jihad answered.

The Brothers started getting blankets, and beers from the G ride as Juelz went over to the van and started pulling little chairs from the back.

"Damn! This is a real live clown van!" Asia jokingly said as Juelz was pulling the stuff from off the back of the van.

Yao looked at Asia and said, "Babe, Could you please go over there and set up our spot on the grass?"

Asia knew that this was Yao's way of saying, "Stay out of him and Mya's shit!"

Asia did what she was told and started to lay the blankets down in an open spot.

The Brothers and Warriors all just fell in line and continued to set up shop. Juelz looked at Mya, who was leaning on the front of the van with her hands crossed over her chest. "This bitch," Juelz said under his breath as he went over to see what was going on with her. Juelz stood in front of Mya, lifted her head up so that she was looking at him, kissed her on the forehead, and asked, "What can I do to make it better?"

Mya looked at Juelz and said, "You are doing everything right big dad."

Juelz looked at Mya with a confused look because he wasn't sure if he was supposed to just take that or think something other than what was said. Mya smiled as she looked at Juelz because she could actually see the way that his mind was also in overthinking mode.

Mya said to Juelz, "So, I guess I am not the only one that overthinks things."

Juelz looked at Mya and she knew that Juelz wanted to throw her in the back of that van and fuck the shit out of her.

Mya ran and playfully jumped into the Warriors' arms. The Warriors were tossing Mya around and Mya was looking around trying to catch a look at Juelz's face, but Mya didn't see him. Mya told the Warriors to put her down and as Mya was sliding out of their grip, Mya turned around and Juelz was standing right in front of her. Mya damn near, shit on herself.

"I see you pregaming, huh?" Mya said to Juelz.

Juelz ignored Mya and kept walking with his Brothers. Mya figured that she wasn't going to kiss his ass, so she headed back to the van to look for the pregnancy test that had accidentally slipped out of her hoodie. It was still in the box, so Mya knew exactly what to look for and where to look. Mya quickly made her way to the back of the van where that little chair was, and she spotted the box over in the corner. Mya grabbed the box and shoved it inside of her hoodie.

Ktru walked over to the back of the van to check on Mya and could see that Mya looked red in the face.

Ktru asked, "What's wrong with you? You alright bitch?"

Mya took a deep breath and said with a smile, "yea bitch, I'm goodie. Just ready to get into this movie!" Mya jumped down out of the van and headed over to the spot where the rest of the gang had set up camp. Mya lay on the ground over in the corner, all by herself. The Brothers looked at Juelz who was chillin' in a chair and Steph said, "Man Juelz, don't start this shit, my boy! We all came out here to chill, relax our minds and have a good time my nigga. Cut this shit out, my man!"

Juelz sucked his teeth, but he did get up and make his way over to lay next to Mya.

Juelz laid down beside Mya, turned over onto his back, and started talking to her while he looked up at the sky. "Look at this shit. It's all chill and shit," he said.

Mya didn't respond, so Juelz said, "I know what the fuck you want yo". Juelz put his pen in his pocket and started tickling Mya. Mya immediately started kicking, and laughing while trying to push Juelz's hands away from her body.

"See, I know what your mean ass needs," he said as Mya leaned over to softly kiss him.

Sklyer came over to them all loudly and said, "Yesss bitch! That's what the fuck I am talmbout. Handle that attitude Juelz!" Everyone started laughing and getting into the spots where they were going to watch the movie.

Jihad and Rock were over in the corner politicking. Mya knew that they were talking about watching the area and making sure they didn't get caught slipping. Jihad and Rock were pointing at certain areas on the River. Jihad and Rock made their way over to where everyone was sitting and as they sat down, the Brothers all received a notification. The Warriors already knew that they were sharing their plan of action. The Warriors started having their own private conversations and then the movie previews started playing. Everyone got quiet and started snuggling up on their partners. Juelz told Mya to get another blanket that was sitting off to the side. Mya already knew that Juelz wanted to get nasty. That was another thing about Juelz, that drove Mya crazy. He was nasty-nasty and down for whatever. He always kept it hot and exciting.

Mya grabbed the blanket and threw it over her and Juelz. Mya laid her head on Juelz's shoulder, went inside his pants, and started stroking his dick. Juelz lay there, moaning low in Mya's ear, and that was driving her crazy. Mya's pussy started getting creamy as she lay there rubbing her clit up against Juelz's thigh while still stroking his dick. Juelz slowly slipped his arm under the covers and went on a hunt for Mya's pussy. Once Juelz's finger finally slid into Mya's creamy, dripping pussy, he whispered in her ear, "Ummmm…. there it is!"

Mya bit her lip, while she moved her body in rhythm with his finger poppin." Mya and Juelz laid their pussy poppin' and dick-stroking each other until they both felt their bodies start to jerk. Juelz lifted his head up just enough so that he could gently bite Mya's lip and pulled her in closer to him. They lay there kissing and stroking one another passionately and they both started to moan in each other's mouths as they gently kissed each other. The vibration of his moan sent Mya first. As she was shaking and cumming all over Juelz's hand, she felt Juelz's warm jizz, running through the cracks of her fingers.

Mya slowly took her hand out of Juelz's pants and slowly licked his cum off of her hand. Juelz lay there looking Mya dead in her eyes while she was doing that and then Juelz slowly took his hand out of Mya's sweats. He put his hand up to his nose and took a deep whiff of Mya's scent. He licked the two fingers that were inside Mya and then he put the remaining fingers up to Mya's face. She grabbed Juelz's wrist and slowly started licking each of his fingers. Mya's leg was still on top of Juelz and when she licked his fingers, she could feel his dick jumping with excitement.

"Down monster", Mya jokingly whispered in Juelz's ear. Juelz wrapped his arms around Mya's neck to hug her and then he playfully pulled her down into his chest.

Mya snuggled up in Juelz's armpit and started watching the movie. Mya really wasn't interested because it was your typical hood movie named, "Stitches."

The gang was about 1 hour into the movie, and it seemed like everybody at the River's phones, received a notification at the same time. It wasn't long before a thousand and one side conversations started and then the Warriors and Brothers, all checked their phones. Their phones all showed the River, along with the movie that was currently playing. Suddenly, gunshots rang out and everyone that was on the grass and in their cars started to scatter. The Brothers all pulled out and started shooting at the black Chevy. The Warriors got low and headed back to the van. Mya turned around to see what the Brothers were doing and Jihad was dead behind them on their ass. Jihad started yelling at the Warriors to jump in the van and then head back to Rock's crib.

Jihad jumped up front with Rainah and started barking orders at her. "Head straight to Rock's house and take Gunther Ave," he said.

Rainah fell in line, and they all rode back to Rock's crib in silence. Jihad and the Warriors were sitting in the van in the back of Rock's house, waiting to hear something from the Brothers.

Finally, Jihad received a FaceTime call. "Yizzo. We are on our way to you. ETA is 5 minutes,"

Rock said. "Coo," Jihad answered.

They all continued to sit in the van in silence and then Skyler sent the Warriors a text that read, "bitch! What the fuck is going on?"

Everyone looked at each other and shrugged their shoulders. Mya was about to send a reply text and then the Brothers pulled up.

Jihad jumped out of the van and the Warriors did the same.

Rock got out and said, "We ain't even going to git into this out here. Let's head down to my basement and figure out what the fuck is goings on!" They all quietly followed Rock into the crib and headed straight to the basement.

As they all filled in downstairs, Yao said, "Alright y'all. We've been going over this shit again and again and keep coming up empty."

The Brothers were all pacing around the basement while trying to figure out what the fuck was going on.

Steph said, "Yea, You right. This shit just ain't addin' the fuck up yo!"

Juelz finally chimed in and said, "Alright den. Everybody stays the night with each other. Rock, go grab them Ring security jawns out the back of your ride, so we can set them shits up."

Rock headed up the stairs to go grab the security system and they all were standing around waiting for their instructions. No one else said anything, so the Warriors followed Rock up the stairs so that they could get in where they fit in.

The Warriors and the Brothers were all pitching in and helping to get the security system set up. Rock and Jihad were giving out instructions on where to place the camera and everyone just played their part without questioning. The cameras were all set up and then Rock checked to make sure that everything was working right and that all the angles were shown.

"Alright bet. We are all good here," Rock said.

Jihad then said, "Bet. Now we can all start heading to the places where we are all staying for the night and set up the security system there also". They all started breaking off into pairs, while Jihad made sure that each Brother had everything needed to hook up their security system.

CHAPTER 22

J uelz and Mya were in the van and Mya said, "We can stay the night at my house. I know Genie is there, but I'mma handle it."

Juelz and Mya headed back to her place and Mya was super relieved that no bullshit had popped off on the way there. Juelz pulled around back and Mya hit the garage door key. Juelz jumped out of the van and told Mya to go get a ladder so that they could start putting the cameras on the outside of the crib. Mya was so over this black Chevy shit, that she couldn't wait to get to the bottom of this shit so that it could be over. Mya grabbed the ladder and then she and Juelz started going around the house, while Juelz placed the cameras.

Juelz was coming down the ladder and when he got to the bottom, he started clapping the debris off of his hands and clothes and then said to Mya, "Let's go inside and take this shit for a run."

Juelz followed Mya inside to the kitchen and then Mya started putting the information that Juelz was giving her, into her cell. After entering all the information, angles of every part of Mya's house started to reel play on her cell.

"Ok, den. We all goodie," Juelz said.

Juelz headed up the kitchen stairs and Mya followed him. Mya had no idea where Genie was and Mya was so burnt out, that she had no intention of going back and forth with Genie if she caught Juelz going into her room.

Juelz flung open Mya's bedroom door, started stripping, and headed straight towards her bathroom. Mya didn't even feel like keeping him company in the shower, so she plopped down on the edge of her bed, breathed heavily, and slipped off her slides and socks. Mya had been through so much shit that day, that she had forgotten all about the anklet that Genie gave her. Mya placed her leg on her bed, started messing with the hanging heart charms, and smiled as she admired her gift. Juelz was coming out of the shower, drying off, and looking at the anklet that had Mya smiling from ear to ear.

Juelz was shaking the towel to dry off his head and then he said, "What nigga you suckin' and fuckin', and trickin' on you?" Mya didn't even let Juelz's petty ass comment phase her.

Mya put her leg down, pulled down her sweatpants leg, and said, "I hope you didn't use up all the hot water." Mya got up and started taking her clothes off and headed to her bathroom. Mya locked the door and went straight for her nose candy stash. Mya opened the linen closet, reached in the back of her washcloths, and pulled out a bag of coke. Mya took the straw out of the bag and took 3 bumps off the end of the cut straw. Mya held her nostrils closed and threw her head back and enjoyed the drip as it traveled down the back of her throat. Mya then hopped into the shower and started washing up. Somehow, Juelz found his way into the bathroom and saw that Mya had forgotten to put the coke stash back and he could be heard taking 2 bumps. Mya pulled the shower curtain back and said to Juelz, "Why you all in my shit. You vulture!"

Juelz took one last bump and then left the bathroom. Mya finished washing off, hopped out of the shower, put her stash back, and then headed out into her bedroom. Mya walked into her bedroom naked, and the coke had her hornier than a muthafucker. Mya walked over to lock her bedroom door, told Alexa to play a fuck song, and then she lay on her bed. Juelz was trying his best not to give Mya any attention, however, Mya started touching herself. Juelz took his pen out of his pocket and started smoking as he sat in Mya's desk chair watching, as she played with her pussy. Mya was stroking her pussy, nice and slow, and then she threw her head back and started moaning.

Juelz couldn't take it anymore, so he placed his pen on Mya's desk and slowly made his way over to the bed. Mya laid on the bed, finger poppin' herself and cummin' all over her fingers and Juelz gently took Mya's finger out of her pussy and sucked all the cum off of her fingers. Juelz climbed on top of Mya and started grinding on her. Mya and Juelz lay in her bed, kissing and grinding and then Mya begged for it.

"Big dad, please, I want to feel you inside me now!"

Juelz just kept grinding on Mya until she just couldn't take it anymore. She aggressively flipped Juelz over onto his back, got up on the back part of her feet, and crouched down over Juelz's face. Mya started to slowly whine her hips all the way down until her entire ass was planted on the top of Juelz's face.

Juelz wrapped his arms around Mya's thighs so that she would not be able to get up off his face. Juelz started sucking the shit out of Mya's pussy, as she aggressively thrust her hips back and forth, on his face. Mya knew that Juelz loved eating her pussy and the moans and slurps that he made while eating her pussy, caused her to cum in his mouth at least 3 times. Juelz kept his arms wrapped around Mya's thighs, as he picked her up and threw her body against the wall. Juelz was still sucking on Mya's pussy as her body was pinned against her bedroom wall. Juelz was sucking the life outta Mya and right before Juelz went in for the finishing move, he threw Mya onto her bed, jumped on top of her, grabbed both of her legs, and wrapped them around his waist. He then buried his head in the side of her neck, and he gave her gentle, long, hard strokes.

Mya's body was in such shock, that all she could do was surrender to Juelz. Juelz was balls deep in Mya and it was at that moment, Mya knew that she could not live without him. Mya would never tell him something like that out of fear of him 'moving differently'. Mya was all in her head, while Juelz was going to town on Mya's tight, wet, dripping pussy. Juelz started talking all types of shit to Mya, while he was 7 ½ inches deep in her. "Damn, baby. I hate the way you got me," he said.

Mya remained silent and started thrusting her hips upward and fucking Juelz back. Juelz pinned Mya down so that she was unable to fuck him back and then he whispered in her ear, "I'm going to git your nasty ass pregnant." Mya sank deeper into Juelz's embrace, and they came together. Mya's legs were shaking and so was Juelz's body, and he just left it in as he lay on top of her. Mya softly started stroking the back of Juelz's head. His drained body lay lifeless on top of her. Mya waited for a minute and then she whispered in Juelz's ear, "Baby, don't ever leave me". Juelz didn't react in the manner that Mya thought he would, instead he just laid on top of Mya, still lifeless. Juelz wasn't pressing the issue, so Mya decided that she was just going to let it go. Juelz finally responded by moving to the left of Mya, telling her to turn around, and then he wrapped his arms around her body. Mya snuggled into Juelz's embrace and then they fell asleep.

CHAPTER 23

Mya didn't have any bad dreams that evening, but for some reason, she was shocked to see Juelz still lying down beside her in the bed that next morning. Mya could smell that Genie was already downstairs cooking, so that meant that she already knew that Juelz was there. Mya pushed Juelz a couple of times, in order to wake him up. On the last push, Juelz woke up, wiping the cold from his eyes.

"Genie has made us breakfast, so you already know what that means," Mya said.

Juelz turned over on his back, sucked his teeth, jumped up to put his clothes on, and then he said, "Mya I love and appreciate Genie babe, but I don't got this shit to do early on a Sunday morning,"

Mya slapped Juelz on his ass and jokingly said, "Come on my nigga. The least you can do is go downstairs and share a hot meal with a woman that already knows all the nasty type shit you be doin' to her granddaughter."

Julez jumped up and started getting dressed. Juelz looked at Mya and said, "See! That's why all you fuckin' Shaw women stay in some shit wit a nigga."

Mya jumped up, slid on her slippers, and put on her house gown.

"Come on nigga. Let's go eat," Mya said.

Juelz and Mya used the back stairs and headed down to the kitchen. Mya was leading the way and Juelz stopped Mya in her tracks by gently grabbing onto her shoulder.

Juelz looked at Mya and said, "We gone talk about the security cameras' that we put up last night and that's ALL."

Mya agreed and continued walking down the stairs, however, she knew that was not the only thing that Genie was going to bring up.

Genie was standing at the stove cooking and as Juelz and Mya entered the kitchen, Genie immediately said, "Ohhhh. So that's what we doing now? Playing my house like it's some sleazy ass motel and then have the nerve to come to eat and don't even greet the cook?!"

"Mo'nin Genie," Juelz said. "Thank you for taking care of breakfast," Mya added.

Genie made Mya and Juelz a plate and then sat their plates on the table. "Y'all, get ya grown ass over here and git some GOOD nutrition in you to start your mo'nin'."

Mya and Juelz sat down at the table and then Genie pulled out a chair next to Juelz. Juelz was trying to ignore Genie, but it was impossible to do that.

"What's up Genie? What did I do wrong this time?" Juelz asked.

Genie grabbed Juelz's face and said, "Look chile, you ain't done nuthin' wrong! What I do want to ask you is, are you ready for all the things that grown-up living doesn't tell you about?"

Juelz ate his eggs as he confusingly looked at Genie, who was all up in his personal space. "To be honest Genie. I have no clue what you are talking about," he said.

Genie got up from her chair, looked at Mya, made eye contact and then she looked back at Juelz and said, "I'm not sure that neither of you are," and walked into the living room. Juelz and Mya looked at each other and finished fucking up their breakfast.

Mya had forgotten all about that she was supposed to go and visit her mom this morning. Mya was eating her breakfast and then she looked at the time on the kitchen clock and said to Juelz, "Babe, I am so sorry. I have to call my daddy and start getting ready to go see Mamma today."

Juelz stabbed at his eggs while looking at Mya and said, "You know what? That shit was kinda shady that you didn't tell me you were going to see ya mom today."

Mya looked at Juelz because she never actually thought that it was a big deal whether she told him or not. "I am so sorry that me not telling you, made you feel a way, but honestly babe, it was like a spur-of-the-moment thing," Mya said.

Juelz got up from the table, scraped the food off the plate that he didn't eat, and then headed back upstairs.

"Where are you going Juelz? Let's talk about this shit babe," Mya low-key yelled.

Mya punched on Juelz's back, as he walked up the backstairs. Juelz was headed to grab the van keys out of her bedroom, and he gave Mya absolutely no reaction as she was still punching him. Juelz grabbed his things and headed towards the backstairs so that he could go out to the garage and get in his van. Mya followed Juelz all the way to his van, while still trying to plead her case, but Juelz didn't say a word. Genie must have heard the fool that Mya was making of herself, so she sat at the kitchen garage door and yelled out to Mya to get her ass in the house now.

Juelz hopped in the van, looked Mya in the eyes, shook his head, and pulled off. Mya was pounding on the van as Juelz drove off, and Genie could be heard in the background saying, "Chile, get your whopped ass in this house!"

Mya closed the garage door and headed into the house. Mya looked at Genie as she passed her and softly said, "I think you meant, get your whipped ass in this house."

Genie sucked her teeth, put her hands on her hips, and said, "Chile, I know you ain't hardly worried about the right word being used to describe yo Juelz happy, ass!"

Mya continued up the backstairs to finish getting ready for her dad to come scoop her.

Mya went and took a few bumps from her secret stash, put her clothes on, and headed to wait outside on the front porch for her daddy to arrive.   Mya sat on the steps, scoping out her surroundings and then she suddenly remembered that her daddy wasn't coming to scoop her, rather his dusty ass wife would be pullin' up. Mya came back to reality and saw that it was her dad's wife, seated in the driver's seat of the Lex. Mya sucked her teeth hard as hell, as she jumped up off the porch and headed towards the car.

"I really ain't got this bitch to do right now," she said under her breath as she got into the back seat.

Mya's dad's wife looked in the rearview mirror at Mya and jokingly said, "Where to madam?"

Mya sucked her teeth and just turned her body to the side and started staring out the window. Ms Geraldine pulled off while saying, "On our way to Mountain Valley. Please leave a generous tip, along with a generous review about your ride with UberBrown, today."

Mya knew that this was Ms. Geraldine's way of trying to connect with her, but she did not respond to her shenanigans.

Mya continued to look out the window and take in the scenery as they drove 1 1/2 hours in silence, to Mountain Valley to see her mamma. They pulled up to the institution and Mya jumped out of the back seat without saying a word to Ms. Geraldine.

Ms. Geraldine stopped Mya as she headed into the building and said, "Mya, I will be in town during your visit. Call me and let me know if I need to be back here earlier than 1 ½ hours." Mya looked at Ms. Geraldine, rolled her eyes, and then shoved her EarPuds into her ears and walked to the entrance. Ms. Geraldine sat there and watched Mya as she entered the building. Once Mya was in the building, she looked out the window and saw that Ms. Geraldine was still outside, as Mya went through the automatic sliding doors, she stuck her middle finger up at Ms. Geraldine. Ms. Geraldine chuckled, beeped the horn, and then pulled off.

Mya took out her earbuds and went to the front desk to let them know that she was there to see Milan Shaw. Mya waited in the waiting room for 20 minutes before someone came out and called her name to head back to her visit. Mya angrily jumped up and followed the man who called her. Mya was led to what looked like a rec room and her mom was seated over at the Chess table. Mya started thinking and saying to herself, "I know Mamma don't want no smoke with Chess because I don't remember the last time I played."

Mya's mom got up and gave her a tight, long hug.

Mya's mom stepped back and said to Mya, "Oh my gosh baby girl. Step back and let mamma look at you!" Mya sheepishly stepped back as her mamma twirled her around while she was hyping her up. "OOOH my lord! My baby girl has grown into a young lady!"

Mya couldn't stop smiling because she forgot how confident Mamma always made her feel. Mya sat down and started kissing Mamma all over her face.

Mamma grabbed Mya's wrist, looked Mya dead in her eyes, and then said, "Oh my god My. (that's what she called Mya when she was either mad or disappointed with her). You're pregnant!" Mya put her head down and Mamma pulled her head back up and said, "Look at me, my love," Tell Mamma what's on your heart."

Mya was trying to muster up the courage to cry, but she couldn't. Mya looked down at the floor and said, "Mamma honestly, being pregnant is the least of all my worries."

Mamma didn't respond, she just kept looking at Mya in her eyes. Mamma put both of her arms around Mya and Mya sank into her embrace and said, "Mamma, I don't know where to start".

Mamma let Mya cry and snot, without interrupting her. Mya looked at her mamma and said, "Mamma, someone has been trying to kill me and my friends since early Friday morning, and neither of us knows what is going on." Mamma didn't respond, she just held Mya tighter and started to rock back and forth. Mamma started to hum that old negro spiritual that Genie was humming earlier yesterday, and Mya just broke into another major crying session. Mamma kept humming and rocking back and forth and then Mya cleared her throat, wiped her tears, and then sat straight up. Mya gathered herself, looked at Mamma, and said, "The Warriors and I received a Snap yesterday, and the story showed our family picture from when we were younger and a scene of a graveyard. Do you remember anything with those things in it?" Mamma's grip loosened up on Mya and Mya became concerned. "Mamma is there something that you are not telling me?" she asked.

Mya's mom rocked back and forth in her rocking chair for about two minutes and then she said, "There is something that you should know."

CHAPTER 24

Mya turned to Mamma and started bouncing her leg up and down as she played around with her hands, waiting for Mamma to tell Mya what she needed to know.

Mamma took a deep breath and then said, "My, there is no easy way to tell you this, so I'mma just gone head and say it."

Mya's leg was still bouncing up and down, a mile a minute, as she waited anticipating what mamma was going to say.

Mamma looked at Mya and then said, "when I was fourteen years old, I was in a relationship with a boy my age and I thought we were going to be with each other for the rest of our lives. I got pregnant and although we were both young parents, we decided that we were going to keep the baby, continue with school, and build a family. The baby was born and all of a sudden, this strong feeling of panic and anxiety came over me, and I could not for the life of me shake that feeling. There I lay in that hospital bed, holding the baby boy that I had just given birth to. I looked at my baby as he was innocently snuggled in my arm, and I turned to his dad and told him that I changed my mind. I wasn't willing to go on with raising our son. His father looked at me and said, "You don't ever have to worry about hearing from me or our son again."

Mya just sat there speechless and overwhelmed. Mamma could see that Mya was going through it, so she grabbed the bottom part of Mya's face, looked her in the eyes, and said, "My, I can't even imagine what you are going through right now, but just know this, what I shared with you, has never come back to rear its head."

Mya didn't know what to think, but she did know that she didn't want to hear that shit. Mya looked at Mamma and said, "Who else knows about this mamma?"

Mamma adjusted herself and said, "Your daddy, Genie, and your Nana."

Mya jumped up out of her seat and started pacing around her mamma. Mamma just sat quietly, rocking back and forth as Mya walked around punching her hands together. Mya stopped pacing and then she looked her mamma in the eyes and asked, "Did y'all even name him?"

Mamma took a second before she answered and then she said, "We named him Mitchell, but I honestly don't know what name his dad chose to put on his birth certificate".

Mya sat back down and said to her mom, "Mamma I have so many questions right now, but I am only going to ask you one that really matters right now. Do you think that my long-lost brother is trying to kill us?" Mamma got up out of her rocking chair, headed over to Mya, and then put her arms around her.

"Mya, I can't sit up here and give you the 100% sure answer that you are looking for, but I will call his dad. I promise you that I will have more information for you the next time that we speak!" Mya looked at her mom, gave her a kiss on the forehead, and headed out of the rec room. Mamma was in the background, calling for Mya to stay, but Mya continued to head towards the exit.

Mya made her way outside to sit on the bench and wait for Ms. Geraldine to pull up, but she peeped that Ms. Geraldine was already sitting in a parking spot in front of the building.

"Thank god," Mya mumbled under her breath as she went to hop in the car.

Mya jumped in the front seat this time; however, she turned her body so that she was facing out the window. Ms. Geraldine looked over at Mya without saying a word, and then she pulled off. Mya angrily shoved her earbuds in her ears because although it was silent, she felt like Ms. Geraldine was holding a conversation with Mya, in her mind. Ms. Geraldine allowed Mya to listen to her music for about 45 minutes and suddenly, she pulled off on the side of the road.

Mya took her AirPods out, looked around, and then confusingly looked over at Ms. Geraldine.

"What's up?" Mya asked.

Ms. Geraldine took a deep breath, turned the car off, and then turned her entire body so that it was facing Mya.

"Look, Mya. I am not sure what this is between you and I, but this has gone on long enough." Mya shrugged her shoulders and avoided eye contact with Ms. Geraldine.

Ms. Geraldine became a little bit more aggressive and then she said, "Fine! We can sit here all day, but I am not moving this car until you and I talk."

Mya sat silent for about 3 minutes before she turned her body towards Ms. Geraldine and then she asked, "Were you fuckin' my dad while my mom was in the mental institution?" Ms. Geraldine took another deep breath and then said, "Look, Mya. Grownup things happened between me, and your dad and I refuse to get into those details with you. I will say this though, when I slept with your dad and got pregnant with the twins, I had absolutely no idea that your dad was married."

Mya just started crying and then Ms. Geraldine said, "Mya, you are, have been, and will always be loved beyond measure. By everyone. I am not asking you to like me, but I am asking for your respect. I have and never will do anything disrespectful towards your daddy or anyone/situation that came before me. Your daddy is your daddy. Me being in his life, has not nor will it ever, affect what he is to you and the bond that you two have. I just want you to show the same respect towards me that I have given to you. Your half Brothers and sisters, as you call them, love you soo much, even though you don't always show them you care. Honestly, Mya, they don't care about that. They love their big sis so much, that you would think that they are twins with you!!" Mya started laughing and Ms. Geraldine started the car.

Ms. Geraldine looked over at Mya and said, "See there! That's the part of Mya that I could wake up to every morning!" Mya was still laughing, and she looked at Ms. Geraldine and jokingly said, "ok...that was a little over the top!" They continued to laugh and as Ms. Geraldine was driving, she looked over at Mya and said, "Sooooo, what's new with you and Mr. Juelz?"

Mya still couldn't believe that she was vibin' this hard with Ms. Geraldine. Mya was caught off guard by the question, and she answered, "we good. He ain't going nowhere!"

Ms. Geraldine chuckled and said, "Oh boy, do I remember it like it was yesterday." "Remember what?" Mya asked.

"Chile, I remember what that puppy love felt like," Ms. Geraldine said.

Mya slid in a joke and said, "Don't blow a brain fuse trying to remember the Days when Dinosaurs roamed!"

"Ha ha ha," Ms. Geraldine replied.

CHAPTER 25

Ms. Geraldine and Mya drove the entire ride back, crackin' jokes, sharing memories about Mya's brothers' and sisters', and talking about where the family was going to vacation for the holidays. Mya received a FaceTime call from Juelz, and she declined it. Juelz immediately sent Mya a text message saying, "There better be a good fuckin' reason why you declined my call. Call me the fuck back ASAP, so that we can talk about what you told me last night"

Mya's whole mood instantly changed, and she became upset all over again. Ms. Geraldine looked over at Mya and could tell that it was Juelz who had her in her feelings.

Ms. Geraldine said, "I'm going to say something to you Mya and I want you to hear my heart when I say this. You are a very beautiful, intelligent, brave young lady. Darlin' you are only 17 years old, and you have the rest of your life ahead of you. Trust me when I say, I don't know what you are feeling, but I have been in your shoes many times before. Juelz is not the be-all to end-all. He is just familiar to you and that brings you comfort. Live your life, Mya.

Don't let anybody break your stride. You got to keep on moving regardless of what happens in life."

Mya sat silently as she thought about what Ms. Geraldine had just said to her.

Mya looked at Ms. Geraldine and said, "I don't care what nobody says. You alright wit me!" Mya and Ms. Geraldine started laughing and then Ms. Geraldine received a call on her car Bluetooth.

The voice of Mya's dad came across the speakers. "Glad to see ya'll didn't kill each other," He playfully said.

"No Daddy! We're all good," Mya said.

"Hey, handsome. We actually talked, hashed a few things out and everything is all good," Ms. Geraldine said.

"Good, good. That is music to my ears. Hearing two of the most important ladies in my life getting along," Mya's dad said.

Mya's dad started having a conversation with Ms. Geraldine. "Hey hone, I wanted to let you know that the babysitter dropped the children off at Genie's because she had a family emergency. How far out are you so that I can call and give Genie an ETA?"

"Ahhh, I should be there in about 30 minutes," Ms. Geraldine responded.

"OK. I'll call and let her know. I have to get back to work now. You guys drive safe, and we'll talk later."

Right before Mya's dad disconnected the call, Mya yelled out, "Daddy we need to talk."

"Ok, baby girl. Gotta go. Love ya'll", and then he hung up.

Mya felt a little disappointed because she really wanted to have a conversation with her dad about what her mamma had told her. Mya looked down at her phone and decided to reply to Juelz's text. Mya began to text, "I am omw home now. I will call you in an hour and then you can come through." Mya looked down at her phone and noticed that the three dots on her text message screen had been floating for about 3 minutes. When she received a text back, all Juelz replied was, "Cool."

This made Mya angry as hell, but she didn't want to let Ms. Geraldine see her sweating Juelz again, so Mya blocked him. Mya looked over at Ms. Geraldine and said, "You ain't gonna be all in your feelings if I put my AirPods in are you?" Ms. Geraldine waved Mya off and Mya put her air pods in and started scrolling through social media.

"Lemme check dis nigga's Insta," Mya said to her herself. Mya went to lurk on Juelz's Instagram page, and lo and behold, Juelz had posted a picture of The Brothers at a bowling alley. Mya scrolled further down the page and saw The Valley Chicks in the back of the bowling alley. Mya's blood started to boil, and she checked the time and saw that she was only 10 minutes away from home. Mya angrily sent the Warriors a group text and let them know what she had seen on his page. Neither of them answered her text and as Mya continued to scroll down his page, she could see the Warriors over in the arcade area. At this point, Mya was so angry that if she owned a gun, she would probably go shoot up the place.

Mya and Ms. Geraldine pulled up to Genie's house and before the car came to a complete stop, Mya jumped out of the car and ran towards the crib. Mya burst through the front door. Genie and her younger siblings were all in the family room, and Mya didn't say anything to anyone. She ran up the stairs to her bedroom, slammed her bedroom door shut, and quickly called the Warriors on a FaceTime call. Mya called twice before the Warriors answered.

"You muthafuckin' bitches are shady as hell!!" she yelled.

"Girl. calm your goofy down," Ktru said.

"We already know what you talmbout bitch, and it ain't even like that," Skyler said.

"We actually came down here on a humbug because we all peeped the Brothers' page and saw that those white Valley cunts were here," Asia said.

Mya looked at the Warriors and said, "oh, okay. Cuz a bitch was bout to come through and get active."

"Later for all that bitch. You comin' through or nah?" Rainah asked.

"You bitches could have at least airdropped me the situation," Mya snapped.

"Bitch, we were more focused on getting her ASAP. We knew that you were visiting your mom, so we didn't hit you," Ktru said.

Mya sucked her teeth and asked, "How long have y'all been there?"

Asia replied, "We have been here for about a half."

"Alright. Imma get Ms. Geraldine to drop me off. I'll text y'all when I'm on my way," Mya said.

"Ok bitch. Jus git here," Skyler said.

Ms. Geraldine dropped Mya off in front of the bowling alley, and the Warriors were outside waiting for her.

"Alright, Ms. Geraldine. Thank you for the ride. Love you, Gerald. Love you, Jackson. Love you, Mariah," Mya said to her younger half-siblings as she got out of the car. Gerald and Jackson were Mya's' younger twin brothers and Mariah was her younger sister.

Mya ran over to the Warriors, and Asia screamed out to Mya, "Pause bitch. Don't go up in there trying to get active with nobody." Mya ignored Asia and walked into the bowling alley. Mya's first mission was to locate Juelz. The Warrior were all trying to chat with Mya, but she was so focused on finding Juelz that their voices sounded like the grandmom on Charlie Brown.

Mya spotted Juelz bowling in lane 13 and the Valley Chicks were bowling in lane 14. Mya was walking over towards Juelz, and she peeped that Chloe was all in his face. Mya ran full speed over towards them, jumped up in the air like she was Bruce Lee and karate kicked Chloe in her back. Chloe's body fell into Juelz, and then Mya grabbed Chloe by her hair, snatched her out of Juelz's arms, and flung her onto the floor. The rest of the Valley Chicks came running towards Mya and before Jessica could jump on Mya's back, Ktru came from behind Jessica and punched her in the back of her head. The Valley Chicks and The Warriors were all mixing in the bowling alley. The Brothers were trying to break the Warriors away from the Valley Chicks, and then, all of a sudden, a big brawl broke out. There were chairs, drinks, and food flying everywhere. The employees and adults that were in the bowling alley were all trying to break up random fights.

The Brothers were finally able to break all the Warriors away from the Valley Chicks, and then 12 showed up. "Let's go nigga's," Jihad said. The Warriors and the Brothers headed to the emergency exit. As they were exiting the bowling alley, more cops were showing up. "We'll all meet up at my place," Rainah said.

"Cool," Yao answered. The Warriors jumped in Rainah's whip and the Brothers jumped in Juelz's van. They sped off towards Broad Street, and right before the intersection, the black boxed Chevy came from the right and rammed into the side of Juelz's van. Juelz's van did a 180 spin, and then the Chevy rammed into the back of the van. The black Chevy was behind the van while chasing them down the street. Rainah looked through her rearview mirror and saw that there were two cop cars behind the van and the Chevy.

The black boxed-Chevy veered off to the right, and one of the cop cars started chasing the Chevy. Juelz continued driving the van, and the other cop got behind him and started chasing them. The Warriors thought Juelz was going to stop, but that nigga sped up. "Oh, my fuckin' God!" Mya yelled.

"This nigga is nutty as fuck!" Rainah said.

"Y'all know that at least one of them nigga is strapped. That's prolly why they are not stopping," Asia said.

"Pull over to the side, let them pass, and follow them bitch!" Skyler yelled.

"You already," Rainah said. Juelz was dippin' in and out of alleyways and side streets. The Warriors were cheering them on as they were getting away from 12. The chase was now on Cranberry and Apple Ave, and then an 18-wheeler just happened to run a light, which allowed Juelz to get away and block the cop in.

CHAPTER 26

Rainah FaceTimed Rock to see where they were. The Brothers and the Warriors met up on Arney Street. When the Warriors made it to Arney Street, Steph told them to stay in the car. The Brothers walked over to Rainah's beamer, and Steph gave his house keys to Skyler and told them to go there ASAP. Mya was almost in tears as she looked at Juelz and asked him,

"Are you okay, babe?". Juelz did not answer Mya, and this time, for some reason, she did not feel some type of way.

All the Brothers' except Juelz, gave their girl a kiss. Mya didn't even react; rather, she pulled out her phone and texted Dylan. Juelz saw what Mya was trying to do, and he reached through the window and tried to snatch her phone out of her hand. Everyone couldn't believe that Mya and Juelz were acting like kids in the midst of all the bullshit that was poppin' off. Yao pushed Juelz back to the van and told him to get in the passenger seat so that he could drive. The Brothers all loaded up in the van and headed down Arney Street and then BAM! A U-Haul truck rammed into Juelz and the crew, pressing his van up against a building, and then someone from the U-Haul started opening fire. The Warriors were still parked on the side of the street as they witnessed this shit unfold.

The Brothers started bussing back at the U-Haul, and then four guys wearing clown masks and gray hoodies jumped out of the U-Haul truck and started scattering in different directions. The Warrior waited for about 5 minutes before they hopped out of Rainah's ride. They all ran over to Juelz's van and Jihad flung open the van door and told Ktru to hop in the driver's seat of the U-Haul.

"Back this shit up!" Jihad yelled.

Whoever was in the Uhaul, had left the keys in the ignition when they jumped out. Juelz reached inside of his van glove compartment and handed Ktru a pair of latex gloves.

Ktru put on the gloves and quickly backed the U-Haul off the van. Amazingly, Juelz's van was still drivable, so Steph told the Warriors to keep with the original plan and head to his place. The Brothers had to go stand on business. Without question, the Warriors all headed back over to Rainah's ride and skeeted off towards Steph's crib. The Warriors were all still in shock, so not much was being said among them. Mya then received a text message from Dylan and the text read, "where are you. I need to see you?" Mya texted him back and told him that now wasn't a good time, but Dylan was not taking no for an answer.

Mya asked Rainah to drop her off at home because she had something important to take care of. The Warriors knew that Mya was up to something, but no one was trying to get into with her at this time. Rainah dropped Mya off at home and as Mya was walking towards her crib, she looked over to the left and saw Dylan parked on the opposite side of her street. Mya quickly headed to his car and plopped down on the passenger seat. Mya looked at Dylan with a disgusted look on her face.

"What's wrong with you?" he asked. Mya took a deep breath and asked him what the issue was.

"I heard about that bullshit that popped off at the bowling alley", Dylan said.

"This nigga got ya head that fucked up that you out her fighting white bitches now?" Mya stared at Dylan and because she didn't have any energy to argue with him, she said, "Is there a point to all of this Dylan?"

"I think I know who had something to do with your little nigga getting kidnapped". Mya looked at Dylan and didn't even flinch and said,

"Nigga what the fuck is you talmbout?" "The streets is going to talk, Mya" he said. "Whatever nigga", she replied. Mya didn't know whether this nigga was fishing or if he actually knew something, but she wasn't bout to give up any tapes.

"Look Dylan, I have to go", Mya said.

Mya reached for the door handle so that she could get out, and then he grabbed Mya by her arm, pulled her back into the car and started kissing her. Mya put up a slight fight, but eventually she gave in because she remembered that Dylan was the nigga that took care of her financially. Dylan pulled down his zipper, pulled his dick out and Mya started giving him some sloppy toppy. Dylan and Mya never had sex because Mya was 17 and Dylan was 20. Mya didn't really want to suck his dick; however, she needed two things from him: money and information. Mya braided her braids back, leaned over and then started putting that work in. Dylan grabbed the back of Mya's head and started to slowly push her head deeper down onto his dick. Mya was saved by the bell when Dylan's phone rang.

"Shitt man. Got damn! Who the fuck is this?" Dylan angrily said.

Mya sat up so that Dylan could take the call and instead of talking, Dylan texted a response to whomever was on the other line and then he hung up. Dylan pulled up his zipper, went into his pocket and handed Mya $1000. Mya snatched the money out of his hand

and got out of his car. Dylan rolled the window down and said to Mya,

"we still have some unfinished business". Mya stuck up her middle finger, walked into her crib and ordered an Uber to Steph's crib. As Dylan pulled off, he started chuckling and blew Mya a kiss.

"Dickhead", Mya said to herself.

Mya started walking into her house, while looking down at her phone to order an Uber. Mya's order for an Uber was interrupted by a FaceTime call sneaky link 2.

"Oh my fucking god!" Mya cried out.

"What the fuck is all this about?" she asked herself.

Mya had never experienced hearing from the both of them in one day.

"Something is the fuck fishy", Mya said to herself. Mya answered the phone unbothered,

"What's up?" she asked. the link answered,

"you boo". Mya rolled her eyes up in her head and then said, "listen on some real shit, I really don't have time for this right now".

"Did I do something wrong", the link asked.

"Nawh, I just got a lot going on right now. Let me hit you later", Mya said.

"Before I let you go, I just wanted to know when you started fighting over niggas. That shit is all over the Gram". Mya breathed heavily and said,

"yo, you buggin' and I don't have time for this shit right now".

"Respect. Just know, Mya, we are not done having this conversation", the link said.

As Mya was disconnecting from the call, her Uber pulled up. Mya jumped in the Uber and then she got a FaceTime call from Juelz.

"Where you at yo?" he asked her. "I'm in an Uber on my way there now," she answered. Juelz said nothing and then hung up the phone. "Fuck! Could this evening get any worse?" Mya said to herself. Mya was about 5 minutes away from Steph's crib when she received a call from an Unknown number. Mya hesitated to answer it, but with all the shit that had been going on, she didn't want to take any chances.

"Speak," Mya said as she answered her phone.

"Now, what kinda way is that to answer ya phone?" Mya's mamma jokingly asked. Mya took a deep sigh of relief and then said,

"I'm so sorry, mamma. I had no idea who this might be".

"That's alright, baby. I am sneaking a call in any way because I just wanted to tell you that I found out that your Brother's name has not been changed.

It is still Mitchell", Mamma said.

Mya knew that she couldn't chat with her mamma about this situation, so she just told her thank you and then hung up. Mya didn't have any time to think about what her mom had just told her because the Uber was in the back of Steph's house.

Mya jumped out of the Uber and headed into Steph's crib. Juelz was outside on the balcony, smoking a wood. As Mya walked up to the house, Juelz looked at Mya with the look of death.

"Why the fuck is you staring at me like that?" she asked him. Juelz just kept staring at Mya, and she waved him off and walked into the house. The gang were all sitting in Steph's family room talking about what the Brothers did when they left the scene. Juelz came in the house and asked Mya,

"Where the fuck you go, Mya?" "Juelz, really?" she said. Juelz grabbed Mya by the back of her neck and pushed her into the kitchen. No one saw this because he yoked her up in the small hallway that divides Steph's kitchen and his family room.

Mya aggressively yanked away from Juelz's grip as she looked at him like he had lost his mind. "What the fuck is wrong with you?" Mya snapped at Juelz.

"You are what's fucking wrong with me yo!" Juelz answered.

"Why the fuck you playin' wit me, Mya?"

"What are you talking about?" Mya tried to innocently ask him. "Why the fuck did you go home?" Mya sucked her teeth, turned her back to Juelz, and started walking towards the room where everyone was. Juelz grabbed Mya by the back of her neck again, threw her up against the wall, and smacked the shit out of her. Mya was in such shock that he had actually hit her again. She did nothing.

Juelz had one hand around Mya's neck as she was pinned on the wall. Juelz took his other hand and put it inside of Mya's pants. He pulled her panties to the side, stuck one of his fingers in her pussy, pulled it out, and smelled it. Juelz doing this to Mya made her so mad, that she was able to push him off of her, slapped him in the face and headed to where everyone was. As she was walking into the family room, Juelz said to her, "You gonna regret this, Mya."

Mya entered the family room before Juelz and surprisingly, no one had any idea of what just jumped off in the kitchen.

"Welcome bitch", Skyler said to Mya.

"What did I miss?" Mya asked.

"Pretty much, all y'all need to know is the U haul has been destroyed, and Juelz's van has been torched," Rock said.

"What's our next move?" Yao asked the gang.

Steph answered, "For one, we got school tomorrow so there ain't too many moves that we can make right now ".

"Why can't we?" Ktru asked."

"You know it's homecoming week, and Jihad and Juelz have a big game tomorrow," Yao answered. Jihad and Juelz were on the football team, and they were up to play against the High's biggest rival, tomorrow evening. "Yea, you right," Ktru said.

"Aight den. I'm ready to go back to the crib", Mya said.

"Right", Ktru said as she got up from the couch and started checking for her car keys. The gang all started to get up so that they could bounce and as they were headed out to get into their rides, Asia secretly pulled Mya to the side and whispered to her,

"I jus want you to know that I saw that shit that happened between you and Juelz". Mya looked at Asia and asked,

"Do you know if anyone else seen it?"

"Nawh. everybody was focused on talking about the situation that just happened, "Asia replied.

CHAPTER 27

Mya didn't say a word. She continued to walk out to Ktru's car because she felt so embarrassed. Asia gently stopped her and asked Mya to turn around and face her.

"How many times has that happened?" Asia asked.

With her head bowed Mya whispered, "This is the second time that he actually hit me".

Asia picked up Mya's head, looked her in the eyes, and said, "If you don't leave that nigga alone Mya, something worse is going to happen to you".

Mya kissed Asia on the cheek and walked outside to get in the car,

Ktru drove all the Warriors to their destination, in silence. Mya was the last to be dropped off. The Warriors all got out of the car without saying a word as they each were dropped off. Mya hopped into the front seat and blankly stared out the window. Mya could feel that Ktru was looking at her on and off.

Mya continued to stare out the window, she sucked her teeth and annoyingly asked, "what you gotta say now bitch?"

Ktru could be heard taking a deep sigh and then she replied, "Mya I hope you know that we all saw what Juelz did to you".

Mya did not respond, so Ktru kept talking, "I know that you are tired of us telling you this, but seriously Mya, we are all scared about what could happen. You know these niggas down here have been known for taking out they girl".

Mya still remained quiet for a minute and then she answered, "maybe it would be best if he did off me".

"Oh, my fucking god!" Ktru yelled. "Why would you say some dumbshit like that? What the fuck is really going on with you Mya?"

Mya waited for a minute before she answered. "I haven't had a chance to tell y'all this yet, but when I went to see my mom yesterday, she told me that she had a son with a guy she was in a relationship with when she was 14 years old. She then went on to tell me that her and this guy had made plans to keep the family together, but mom immediately changed her mind when she had him and then she signed over her parental rights to the baby's dad".

Ktru was in such shock that she didn't even know what to say.

"Damn friend!" Ktru whispered. "That is some fucked up shit to just be finding out. Did she tell you anymore about him? Like what's his name? Is he still alive?"

Mya shrugged her shoulders and said, "The only thing she told me is that his name is Mitchell. TBH,

I know that she is not telling me something and that is what is fucking me up."

"Is there anything that I can do, friend?" Ktru asked Mya.

"Nawh, I'm goodie", Mya replied. Ktru slowly started driving as they approached the Front of Mya's house.

Ktru and Mya sat quietly in the car for a minute and suddenly Ktru leaned over and kissed Mya on the lips. Mya's body jerked back as she said to Ktru, "Bitch! What the fuck is you doing?" Rainah said nothing as she stared at Mya until Mya then leaned over and kissed Ktru back. They kissed for about 2 minutes before Mya gently pushed Ktru back and said, "Bitch. The last time that happened, we both agreed that would be our first and last time doing that."

Ktru looked at Mya and said, "yeah you right sis. That's my bad. I was outta pocket for that." Mya gathered herself and started to get out of the car and she replied, "Don't worry about it, friend. We have been through a lot of shit this weekend, so I understand the pressure. We all good baby". Ktru and Mya started laughing. "Whateva bitch", Ktru said as Mya got out and she pulled off.

Mya was walking into her house and the Warriors had agreed to call it a night, however, Mya got an invite to a homecoming house party. Everyone at school was talking, tweeting and posting about it. The Warriors decided that they were only going to go if the Brothers didn't go. There was also a Frat party that same night, at Clingmore University and the Brothers were invited, so they decided to go to the frat party.

When the Warriors arrived that evening, they were already fucked up. Mya and Ktru were holding onto each other, as they stumbled inside the house. Rainah, Skyler and Asia had walked in the house, before them. The Warriors were over their drunk behavior, so they decided to go ahead of them. Mya and Ktru were going up the stairs and Ktru missed a step and they fell into the grass while laughing. When they fell, Mya landed on top of Ktru. They looked at each other and could not stop laughing. They were still laughing as Mya tried to get up off of Ktru and as soon as she was about to stand straight up, she fell back down on the ground, and this caused Ktru to land on top of her.

The laughter stopped and now they were looking confusingly into each other's eyes. Ktru lowered her head and kissed Mya. Mya hesitated for a moment and then she kissed her back. The two of them were laying on the ground kissing and suddenly, the other Warriors came outside yelling at them.

"You drunk bitches need to get y'all self together", Skyler yelled. Asia pulled Ktru off of Mya and Skyler and Rainah started helping Mya up off the ground.

Afraid that they had caught them kissing, Mya decided to check their temperature by asking,

"What the fuck is you talmbout bitch? We were laughing and walking up the steps. Ktru missed a step and we both fell on the ground". Asia replied,

"that's what we are talking about bitch. Y'all all out here on the grass witcha asses out shit. Doing the most".

 Mya was relieved that the Warriors didn't see them kissing.

Mya wrapped her arm around Skyler's neck, Rainah wrapped her arm around Krtu's neck, and they entered the party. The house was filled with raging hormones, high and drunk, teenagers. Mya leaned over and shouted into Skyler's ear, that she was about to go find the bathroom. Ktru insisted on going with Mya, but Mya wanted to go alone because she had plans to do a few lines.

 "Bitch I got it!" Mya snapped. Ktru looked at Mya and could tell that if she kept pressing the issue, then Mya would start doing the most.

"Ok bitch. We'll be in the kitchen", Ktru answered. Ktru headed towards the kitchen as Mya pushed her way through the crowded living room, in search of the stairs.

CHAPTER 28

Mya was heading up the stairs and she felt a smack on her ass. Mya turned around ready to set it off and she noticed that it was Ktru. Mya sucked her teeth, turned back around and continued up the steps.

"What bitch?" Mya annoyingly said to Ktru. Ktru didn't say anything until they got up the stairs.

Ktru then said, "Bitch you already know they weren't going to let you be up here by yourself, besides, a bitch has to pee." Mya breathed deeply and said,

"Whateva bitch. Help me find the bathroom." Ktru and Mya walked around the upstairs, opening different doors in search of the bathroom.

"Oh my god!" Mya yelled as she opened one door. Ktru ran over to see what Mya was looking at and it was a gang of people having an orgy.

"Damn! That's how y'all giving it up?" Ktru jokingly said to them.

One of the boys in the orgy, turned around, looked Ktru in the eyes, started swinging his stiff dick, from left to right and said, "You want some?" Ktru and Mya looked at each other, slammed the door and burst out laughing.

The house had about 10 closed doors, but Mya finally found the bathroom.

"Over here bitch. Hurry up. I gotta pee!" Mya yelled to Ktru.

Ktru sped walked over to the bathroom and before Ktru could close the door, Mya was squatting over the toilet pissing.

"Damn bitch" Ktru jokingly said.

Mya finished her business, washed her hands and pulled out her stash.

"Yessss bitch. Let's git this party started" Ktru excitedly said.

Mya put the coke on the sink, divided it up into four lines and Mya and Ktru handled their business.

Mya bent over to take the first line and it hit her so hard that she jumped back and said.

"Shit!" Ktru looked at Mya and said, "Damn bitch it's like that? Lemme hit this shit" Ktru took her line and did the same thing.

"Shit!" Ktru yelled. They both started laughing and Mya went down to take her last bump. As Mya bent over to snort the coke, she felt something wet in between the crack of her ass. Mya jumped with shock, turned around and Ktru was in a squatted position.

"What the fuck bitch? You buggin'!" Mya yelled.

Ktru stood up face to face with Mya and looked her in the eye.

"Lemme show you something," Ktru said to Mya as she softly ran her finger up and down her inner thigh.

Mya didn't have on any panties and although Ktru was her best friend, she never looked at her in a sexual manner. Ktru's warm kisses and gentle touch, caused Mya to become aroused. Mya leaned her head to the side to make it easier for Ktru to kiss on her neck. Ktru continued to gently kiss on Mya's neck as Mya began to run her fingers through Ktru's hair. There was a plush bench located in the corner of the bathroom. Ktru slowly and gently started to back Mya into the direction of the bench. Mya sat back on the bench and Ktru pulled up Mya's shirt, took off her bra and started sucking on her titties.

The coke made Mya's arousal 10X stronger. Ktru could feel that Mya's body was still kind of tense. Ktru stood up, straddled Mya and whispered in her ear.

"sit back, relax and enjoy the ride." Ktru started to gently kiss all over Mya's neck, titties, stomach and then made her way down to Mya's pussy. Mya instantly opened up her legs and Ktru gently kissed between her inner thighs. As Ktru was kissing on Mya's inner thighs, she extended both of her arms and started playing with Mya's titties. Mya's body became covered with goosebumps as she softly moaned with pleasure.

Mya's moans were turning Ktru on so much that she stood up and took her clothes off. Ktru straddled Mya. Mya raised her head up off of the back of the bench and started kissing on Ktru's neck while sucking her titties. Ktru then took her right index finger and gently slid it into Mya's dripping wet pussy. Ktru became aroused because of the warmness and wetness of Mya's pussy. Ktru started thrusting her pelvis against Mya's pelvis, causing both of their pussy clits to become stimulated. They began to passionately kiss as their clits rubbed against each other. Ktru moaned in Mya's mouth which caused them to begin cumming. Ktru threw her head back in ecstasy as Mya grabbed the back of her hair and started sucking on her titties.

Ktru's finger was still inside of Mya, and she could feel her pussy walls tighten. Mya was about to cum. Ktru started to thrust her hips back and forth, a lil faster and harder. They both moaned in excitement. As soon as they were about to cum, there was a loud bang on the bathroom door.

Mya and Ktru jumped up off of the bench, hurriedly put their clothes back on and then Ktru yelled,

"Someone is in here". Some unknown voices could be heard outside of the door banging on the door and saying,

"our girl is sick. We need to get in there ASAP". Ktru made sure that she and Mya had gathered themselves and then went to open the bathroom door.

Three girls burst through the door. Two ran to the sink to throw up and the other one slid on the floor to throw up in the toilet. Mya looked at them, then looked at Ktru and said, "come on bitch. Let's git the fuck up outta hea".

They headed downstairs and headed to the kitchen. The Warriors could be spotted dancing with some guys, over in the corner. Mya and Ktru walked over to them like nothing had ever happened between them.

"Damm bitches!" What the fuck took y'all so long?" Asia asked.

Without hesitation Mya said, "damn bitch! Can't a bitch throw up?" Asia waved Mya off and continued dancing. Suddenly, Sukihanna's song named 'Hoodrat' came on and the Warriors started yelling and cheering as they made their way to the living room. Mya instantly went live as the Warriors started dancing with people around them.

Mya raised her phone up in the air, started bouncing her ass, chucking up the deuces with her tongue stuck out as she went live. The Warriors saw that Mya went live and they crowded around her, looked into her phone and started doing the same thing that Mya was doing. "Yea y'all know the vibes. Warriors bitches. Yea we outchea! If you ain't here, where y'all atttt?" Mya yelled.

The party was filled with laughter, enjoyment, smoke and good vibes. The Warriors were dancing and enjoying themselves and Mya felt someone come behind her and start grinding.

Mya bent halfway over and started twerking and when she didn't feel the stiffness of a dick, she turned around to see what the fuck was goings on. Mya turned around and faced sneaky link 2, whose name is Sam. Mya felt embarrassed and angry because it was Sam (which is short for Samantha. Samantha was a super stud). The Warriors had no idea that Mya was bisexual, and she wanted to keep it that way. Mya angrily pushed Sam out from the crowd and into the kitchen. Sam had a wood in her mouth and was smiling the whole time Mya was pushing her.

"What the fuck are you doing yo?" Mya shouted at Sam. Sam smirked and said, "What you mean? I was trying to get my dance on." Sam replied.

"You buggin yo. I told you that my girls don't know about us, and I don't want them to", Mya snapped.

"Mannn, fuck all dat! Sam said. "I'm tired of being your fucking little gay secret".

Mya looked at Sam with disgust and said,

"I don't fuckin' know why you trynna switch up bro. I told you before we ever hooked up that the only way that we could git down is if it always stayed strictly between us." Sam sat there quiet, smirking as she hit the wood. Sam blew the smoke into Mya's face and then said,

"Yea, well, that shit different now".

"What the fuck is that supposed to mean?" Mya asked Sam.

"It is what it is," Sam said as she walked away and disappeared into the crowd.

Mya was left standing in the kitchen with a stunned expression. "What the fuck is wrong wit des muthafucka's? Mya said to herself.

Mya popped an MDA, picked up her drink and headed back to find the Warriors. Mya spotted the Warriors over in the dining room area where they were playing beer pong. Asia and Ktru were staring at Mya as she was approaching.

"Everything aight bitch?" Asia asked.

Mya rolled her eyes up in her head, sucked her teeth and said,

"It ain't shit". Skyler was side-eyeing Mya as she said,

"Yea. we hope so bitch!" Mya looked at Skyler and put up her middle finger.

Mya went over to start a conversation with someone she knew from school and as she walked towards the person, she could feel that Ktru was low-key staring at her.

Mya said to herself, "I hope this bitch don't start tweaking like Dylan and Sam. Ktru is my muthafuckin A one day one." Mya started politicking with the person she knew from school, and she felt her phone vibrate.

"Hol up," Mya said. Mya read her text and it was from Ktru. The text read,

'Meet me out in the kitchen so I can go pour us some drinks. Mya sucked her teeth and then told the person she was talking to that she would holla at them later.

Ktru was headed towards the kitchen, and Mya caught up with her and linked arms with her. Mya didn't feel no type of way about what happened between them, and she didn't want Ktru to start moving weirdly because the Warriors would know that something was wrong. Mya and Ktru entered the kitchen and waited until everyone had cleared out. "Whassup bitch?" Mya said to Ktru. "Who was that?" Ktru asked.

Mya knew who she was talking about, but she played dumb.

"Who the fuck you talmbout bitch?" Mya asked.

Ktru looked at Mya like she was crazy and said, "Bitch the games you play. You know who the fuck I'm talmbout," she said.

Mya sucked her teeth and then said, "Oh. I know her from school."

"This is the first time the Warriors and I have seen you talk to her," Ktru said.

 "Bitch! Just because you bitches are my girls doesn't mean that y'all know everybody I the fuck know. Da fuck?" Mya snapped.

Mya put her cup down, looked at Ktru, and said,

"Seriously, girl. I hope what happened between us doesn't change our friendship. You are my fucking girl, and that was just sex." Ktru stood quietly as she stared at Mya, then she said.

"Yea. You right bitch. I'm buggin'." "Bestie's?" Mya said to Ktru.

Ktru looked at Mya, started laughing, and then they hugged it out.

"Come on bitch. Let's go back out there and continue to turn the fuck up!" Mya yelled.

Mya and Ktru linked arms and walked back out into the crowd. As they were leaving the kitchen, Sam came from behind the wall that she was lurking behind. Sam had heard everything that Mya and

Ktru had talked about. Sam was heated as she stood in the corner, smoking the wood and staring angrily at Mya and Ktru as they danced in the crowd. Sam pulled her phone out and sent a text that read, 'Meet me at the spot in 15.' Sam made her way through the crowd and left through the front door. The Warriors were all dancing and having a good time, and then Mya looked over to her left and saw that Sam was leaving the party.

Mya continued dancing, but after about five minutes, something told her to check her phone. Mya checked her phone and saw that she had a text from Sam telling her to meet up in fifteen minutes.

"This bitch!" Mya said to herself. Mya ignored the text and continued turning up. Twenty minutes had passed, and Mya checked her phone only to see that she had 10 missed calls from Sam. "uggh!" Mya said to herself.

"Da fuck do this bitch want?" Mya stepped away to find a quiet area so that she could FaceTime Sam. Mya found a bathroom downstairs and went in there to make the call.

As soon as Sam answered the call, she immediately went off on Mya.

"Why the fuck is you playin' wit me yo? I'm tired of ya shit!" Mya looked at Sam with her face chopped and screwed and said,

"What the fuck is you talmbout? I don't want to meet you. I'm chillin' wit my girls and I ain't ready to be in the house". Mya could tell that if Sam could git to her, she would try to knock her head off of her shoulders. Right before Sam was about to angrily respond to Mya, gunshots were fired.

"What the fuck was that!" Sam yelled.

"Oh my fucking god yo'! Somebody out there shootin'!" Mya yelled. "I gotta go Sam. My girls are out there!" Mya said in a panic.

"Stay your dumb ass where you are. You don't know what the fuck you bout to walk into!" Sam yelled.

CHAPTER 29

"uck dat!" Mya replied. "I'mma hit you back as soon as I find my fuckin' girls!" Sam could be heard still trying to convince Mya not to go out there as Mya disconnected the call. Mya put her ear to the door to see what she could hear. There were no more gunshots, just sounds of people screaming, yelling, and running. Mya slowly opened the bathroom door, squatted down low, and started to quietly move around. Mya FaceTimed the Warriors and neither of them answered.

"Fuck!" Mya quietly yelled.

Mya remained low as she peeked around the kitchen counter. The Warriors were nowhere in sight. Mya FaceTimed the Warriors again. This time, Sklyer answered. Mya whispered as she asked,

"Are y'all ok? Where the fuck y'all at?" Skyler was whispering as she answered, "bitch we in one of these bedrooms. Me and Rainah are under the bed and Asia and Ktru are in the closet."

"Which bedroom?" Mya asked.

"Bitch. I don't fuckin' know," Skyler quietly snapped. "Bet. Turn the location on your phone so I can find y'all," Mya said. Skyler turned her location on and Mya carefully began to go find them. "Got it. OMW". Mya hung up the phone, scoped the scenery out and made her towards the location. Mya quietly made her way to the living room and there was a girl and a guy lying in the middle of the floor. They had been shot. They both were bleeding, but still alive.

"Help me!" The girl cried out. The guy was screaming mad loud because of the pain. Mya went over to them and quietly asked the girl

"Do you know if the person who fired the shots is still here?" The girl shook her head no.

"Sit tight", Mya said. I am going to go find my friends and I am going to call for help". Between gurgles the boy pleaded to Mya,

"Please don't leave us!" Mya looked at the two wounded people lying on the floor and felt bad; however, she knew that her number priority was locating her friends.

Mya grabbed the boy's hand and softly assured him **number one priority,**

"I promise I will not leave before getting y'all help." Mya carefully began to follow the location on her phone.

Mya came upon a light blue door and the location indicator began to go off rapidly. Mya looked up the hallway and down the other side of the hallway to make sure that the coast was still clear. Mya slowly opened the door and softly called out.

"Y'all. It's all clear. Y'all can come out now". The Warriors all began to slowly come out of their hiding places, but they were all still a bit suspect of something else happening. "What's going on out there?" Ktru asked Mya.

"Some dude and this chick got shot and they are lying out on the living room floor bleeding".

"Are they dead?" Asia loudly asked. "Bitch! Keep it the fuck down!" Rainah snapped.

"Naw. they are not dead, but I told them that I would call for help before we left." Mya said.

"Well bitch git activate cuz we got too fuckin' dipset!" Skyler said.

Mya looked around for a house phone so that she could call 911. "I am surprised that 12 ain't here yet," Ktru said.

 Mya spotted a house phone over by the window. "Lemme make this call real quick and then we out," Mya said.

'911, what's your emergency?" The emergency dispatcher asked.

"There is a teenage boy and girl and they have been shot." Mya nervously said.

"Is the perpetrator still in the area?" the dispatcher asked.

"I don't know. Mya said. They are bleeding out on the floor, and they need help ASAP!" Mya hung up the phone and yelled to the Warriors,

 "Yo we out!". The Warriors all dashed out of there and made their way to their ride. "Come on bitches! We do not want to be here when 'dem muthafuckas git here." The Warriors hurriedly jumped in the ride and sped off.

"I'm dropping you bitches off and we will chat later," Rainah explained. Once again, the Warriors were all feeling a way, and no one responded. "This shit jus keeps gittin' nuttier by the fuckin' minute!" Mya thought to herself. Ktru was first to be dropped off and Mya was the last one left in the vehicle with Rainah. Rainah dropped Mya off and did not say anything to her. Mya didn't even feel some type of way because everyone was in their feelings and thoughts about what just happened.

Mya walked into her house and headed straight upstairs. Mya could hear that the twins were home, and she didn't want to be bothered, so she crept quietly up the stairs. Mya walked into her bedroom and hopped right on her phone to check social media. As expected, everyone was talking about what happened at the party. Mya knew that it wouldn't be long before she heard from Juelz. Mya was more concerned about whether those two people that were shot, had survived. Suddenly, Juelz chimed in on Mya's Facetime.

"You aight?" Juelz asked Mya.

"Yea. I'm a lil shook up, but I'll be fine" Mya replied.

"Alright then yo. I got to get ready for this homecoming game tomorrow, so I ain't gone keep you" Juelz said.

Surprisingly, Mya wanted to be left alone so she didn't put up a fight when Juelz tried to get off of the phone.

"Alright yo," Mya nonchalantly said. Juelz sucked his teeth and disconnected the call. Mya sat on the edge of her bed trying to figure out what her next mood was going to be. Mya jumped up, pulled a pregnancy test out of one of her tote bags, and went into the bathroom to pee on the stick.

Interestingly enough, Mya was not as nervous as she thought she would be. Mya stared at herself in the mirror for a quick second, sat down on the toilet, put the stick between her thighs and took the test. Mya placed the completed stick on the edge of the bathroom sink, wiped, stood up to wash her hands and while she was washing her hands, she stood staring at herself in the mirror. Mya's mind started going into overdrive.

'What if I am pregnant? What kind of mom would I be? Would Juelz be mad or excited? He probably would be mad because that would mess up his football scholarship dreams. Will I be like mama and give my child up? What kind of future will I be able to give my baby without an education?'

Mya's overthinking was interrupted by a FaceTime call from her older sister Mychelle.

"Hey sissy pooh," Mya said.

"OMG! Thank God you are okay!" Mychelle yelled. Mya looked at her sister and said, "Damn sis. How the fuc-, I mean, heck did you hear about that so soon?" Mychelle seriously looked at Mya and replied, "You know I got my eyes on my baby sis". Mya didn't know how to feel about what her sister had just said, so instead Mya just said, "Sissy. I really had a long night and I just want to shower and git in bed." "I understand sis," Mychelle said. Mya was about to disconnect from the conversation and somehow, Mychelle caught a glimpse of the pregnancy test that was on the edge of the sink.

"OMFG Mya!" Mychelle yelled.

Mya knew that Mychelle was far from excited because she didn't cuss. Mya tried to play dumb and said, "what is going on with you sissy?"

"Don't play dumb with me Mya. You know exactly what I am talking about," Mychelle answered.

Mya didn't know how to respond because she had not looked at the test results yet. "I'm just trynna be safe and not sorry. No need to trip", Mya said.

"Psst! Safe than sorry? Safe than sorry is using protection. Safe than sorry is taking a Plan B. Safe than sorry is keeping your damn legs closed!" Mychelle yelled to Mya.

Mya had the utmost respect for her older sister, so therefore Mya never got smart with her, regardless of how much her sister may have yelled at her. Without any hesitation, Mya disconnected the conversation and blocked her.

'Bitch got me fucked up! Ain't nobody got time for that shit,' Mya said out loud. Mya placed her phone on the other side of the bathroom sink and slowly began to reach for the pregnancy test.

Mya closed her eyes and slowly started to raise the test up to eye level. Mya took a deep breath in and slowly blew it out as she opened her eyes. Before she could open up her eyes to see the results, one of the twins banged on Mya's bedroom door. Mya got startled and dropped the pregnancy test down the drain.

'You have got to be fuckin' kidding me!" Mya yelled at the top of her lungs.

Mya stormed out of her bathroom, flung open her bedroom door and was all ready to snatch her little brother up, but it was her sister Mychelle.

CHAPTER 30

Mya stared at Mychelle like she had seen a ghost.

"What da fuck?" Mya said.

"Oh. First you hang up on me, block me and now you cussin' at me?" Mychelle said. Mya didn't know how to react, so she just headed over to sit at her desk without saying anything. Mya spun around in her chair, stared at Mychelle and then asked,

"How long have you been in town?" Mychelle walked into Mya's room, closed the door and sat on the edge of her bed facing Mya.

"I haven't been in town," Mychelle mockingly answered. I was actually on the road, on my way down here so that I could go to the homecoming game tomorrow."

Mya sucked her teeth, spun around in her chair and stared at her sister through the mirror. "I dunno sissy. I know that you thought I was going to be surprised but being as though the shit I been through tonight, it jus seem a lil bit sus to me." Mychelle stood up behind Mya as she was seated in her chair, leaned over her and gently wrapped her arms around Mya's neck. With her chin on top of Mya's right shoulder, Mychelle and Mya looked at each other through the mirror and Mychelle softly said,

"I'm sorry sis. I don't want you to be mad at me. I was really trying to surprise you. Do you forgive me for not telling you that I was on my way down here?"

Mya tried her very best to keep being mad at her sister, but she couldn't. Mya playfully sucked her teeth, gently shrugged her shoulders and said,

"You know I can't stay mad at my favorite sister." Mychelle responded by kissing Mya on the cheek and then she plopped back down on the bed. "Soooooo," Mychelle said to Mya.

Am I going to be an aunty or naw?" Mya spun back around in her chair, looked at her sister and said,

"TBH sissy, I don't know because when you just banged on my door, you scared the crap out of me, and I dropped the test down the drain before I could read it."

"Well lucky for you," Mychelle replied as she reached into her bookbag. I stopped by the thrift store on the corner to get another one." Mychelle pulled out another pregnancy test and handed it to Mya.

"Seriously?" Mya playfully asked her sister as she gently snatched it from her.

"Yes ma'am." Mychelle mocked.

Mya headed into the bathroom and Mychelle was right on her heels. Mya turned around and respectfully said,

"Sheesh. I know that inquiring minds wanna know sissy, but can I git some privacy?" Mychelle looked at Mya, sucked her teeth and said,

"I guess".

Mya went into the bathroom, turned on the water and just sat on the toilet waiting to get the urge to pee. Mya was sitting on the toilet for about 10 minutes, and she still didn't use the bathroom. 'Man fuck this,' Mya said as she hopped off the toilet, kneeled down under the sink cabinet, pulled out her hidden 5th of Hennessy and gulped it. Mya didn't want to sit back on the toilet, so she decided to hop in the shower. As Mya showered, all the events that had popped off in her life over the past couple of days, started to run through her mind.

Mya's thoughts were stopped by her sister's knock on the door.

"Sis. Did you fall in?" Mychelle jokingly asked.

Mya turned off the shower, wrapped up in a towel and sat on the toilet.

"Ok sissy. I'm on the toilet now. I will be out in a minute." Mya concentrated on peeing on the stick, however her concentration was broken when she heard a call come in on her sister's phone. The ring tone was that of an old school song called, Always and Forever, sung by a group named Heatwave.

Mya stopped peeing mid pee, quickly and quietly jumped off the toilet and gently placed her ear up to the door to ear hustle. Mya heard Mychelle answer in a whisper voice. "What's up?" Mychelle quietly whispered to the person on the other line. Mya had no idea who was on the other line and what they were talking about, but she just had this gut feeling that something wasn't right about the call. Mya pressed her ear harder on the door, hoping to be able to at least hear if the voice on the other end was a male or a female's. Mya heard Mychelle whisper,

"I told you that I would call you when I had a minute. Why are you being so impatient?"

Mya continued to wait to see if she heard anything that would give her some type of clue or whether she was buggin'. Mya needed to know if her gut was telling the truth. Mya then heard Mychelle say in a whisper voice,

"I'm 'bout to find out now." Before Mya could put her ear closer to the crack of the door to get a better listen, someone banged on Mya's bedroom door. Mya quickly ran back-over to the toilet, grabbed the test and proceeded to pee on the stick. About 5 seconds later, Mychelle burst into the bathroom.

"What the hell?" Mya yelled out not knowing who it was. To Mya's surprise, it was her younger twin sister Myrah.

"What's up brat? Is there a fire or something?" Mya snapped. Myrah rolled her eyes and answered,

"No stupid. Genie told me to come up here and ask you for a pad." Mya looked at Myrah in shock and asked,

"for the fuck who?" Myrah got smart with Mya, and she placed her hands on her hips and said,

"for me genius!" Mya couldn't believe what she was hearing. He ten-year-old sister had a period.

Mya said to Myrah, "alright gimme a minute. Let me finish real quick". Myrah rolled her eyes, sucked her teeth and as she slammed the door she said,

"don't be all day. I need it now." 'This lil winch,' Mya mumbled to herself as she wiped and placed the pregnancy test on her bathroom stand. Mya reached into her bathroom closet and pulled out a pack of pads, threw a robe over her naked body, opened the bathroom door and walked into her room.

Myrah was over at Mya's desk, spinning around in the swivel chair as she chatted with Mychelle. Mya looked at Myrah and asked, "do you even know what to do with these?" Myrah looked at Mychelle, looked at Mya and then looked back at Mychelle and asked Mychelle,

"Where has she been?" as if Mya wasn't standing in the room. "What are you talmbout where I been?" Mya asked her little sister. "Girl, I started my period months ago," her little sister answered.

Mya didn't have any energy to go back and forth with a 10-year-old, so Mya said, "you know what. Take these pads and git the hell out of my room for I do something to you." Myrah hopped out of the chair, snatched the pack of pads out of Mya's hands, and as Myrah slammed the bedroom she said,

"whateva bitch."

 Mya darted towards the door, going after Myrah to snatch her up. Myrah had shut the door before Mya could grab a hold of her. "Ouuu. That lil winch git on somebody nerves!" Mya yelled to Mychelle.

Mychelle laughed as she looked at Mya and said,

"TBH sis. You can't even be mad at her. She only does everything that she sees and hears you do." Mya sucked her teeth and answered,

"Yea. I guess." Mya then remembered the strange behavior that Mychelle was giving when she answered her phone.

"Annyway sissy. Enough about me. Why was you being all secret squirrel on your call earlier?"

Mychelle crunched up her face and looked at Mya like she was speaking a foreign language and said,

"what you talking about sis? Acting secret squirrel how?" Mya looked at Mychelle and blankly stared at her. I guess the way that Mya looked at Mychelle made her uncomfortable because Mychelle then said,

"you are being paranoid sis and trust me, from what you have been through the past couple days, you have every right to be noid." Yet again, Mya didn't have any energy to go back and forth with Mychelle, so Mya let it go and headed to the bathroom to get the pregnancy test.

Mya thought to herself, 'at this fuckin' point, I wouldn't even give a damn if I am pregnant. How much worse can my fuckin' life git?' Mya angrily snatched the pregnancy test off of her bathroom stand and didn't not even look at the results. Mya handed the test to her sister and said,

"here. You read it." Mychelle gently grabbed the pregnancy test, looked at it and said nothing. Mya was already annoyed, so she tried her best not to snap at Mychelle.

"Well?" Mya asked her.

Mychelle was still quiet as she turned the results so that Mya could see them. Mya dropped down onto her bed in disbelief.

"I can't fuckin' believe this shit," she said. Mya was indeed pregnant.

Mychelle scooted closer to Mya and wrapped her arms around Mya. Mya was so numb that she didn't really know what to do. Mychelle sat comforting Mya in silence for about an hour and then Mya drifted off to sleep. Mychelle softly gave Mya a forehead kiss, gently and slowly laid Mya back onto the bed, placed the covers over her, turned off all the lights, grabbed the pregnancy test and quietly left Mya's room.

CHAPTER 31

The next morning, Mya was awakened by chirping birds. Mya laid in the bed for a few minutes before she got up to get ready for her school day. As she laid in her bed, Mya took a few deep breaths because her thoughts immediately started to take charge of her mind. Mya started to encourage herself.

"Come on girl. You gotta calm down. Everything is going to be alright. We gone to take this shit step by step and day by day like we always do.' Mya took a deep breath, sat up on the side of her bed and grabbed her phone off the nightstand.

To Mya's surprise, she didn't have any missed calls or texts, however she had mad DM's. Mya then remembered that the school pep rally was taking place during 2nd period, and the homecoming game was later on that afternoon.

'Fuck,' Mya cried out as she jumped up off of her bed and headed towards her bathroom. As Mya started brushing her teeth, she started to look around the bathroom for the pregnancy test that she had taken last night, but she couldn't find it.

Mya spit the toothpaste out of her mouth, tossed the toothbrush into the sink and started checking her bathroom and bedroom for that pregnancy test. Mya tossed all the covers off her bed while shaking them out. She threw her pillows onto the floor, checked underneath her bed, on her desk and nightstand. Mya stood in the middle of her room feeling crazy and then suddenly, she received a FaceTime call from Ktru.

"Hey sis. I'll be ready in 5 minutes, I promise," Mya quickly said.

"Ok. see you in a few," Ktru replied.

Mya headed to the bathroom to finish brushing her teeth. She washed her face, threw her braids up in a ponytail, and quickly rubbed moisturizer over her body. Mya put on a school jersey that had Juelz's last name and jersey number on the back of it, a pair of ripped jeans along with her Jordan 11s, and then headed downstairs. Mya suddenly remembered that she had forgotten her phone, and as she headed back into her room to grab it, Genie came out of her room and said,

"When you come back in this house, you and I need to have a conversation."

The fact that Mya's life had been one shit show after the other; she had no idea what Genie already knew and wanted to talk about.

"OK, Genie," Mya answered as she darted down the stairs and out the front door. Just as Mya walked down the last step, Ktru was pulling up in front of Mya's house. Mya noticed that none of the other Warriors were in the car.

'It's too early in the morning for this shit,' Mya said under her breath. Mya forced a smile as she walked up to get into the car.

Mya could tell that Ktru's energy was off. She knew that something was wrong with her girl. Mya turned to Ktru and softly asked,

"Is everything okay, friend?" Ktru burst into tears. Mya leaned over to hug Ktru, and that's when Ktru answered,

"Rainah is in the hospital." Mya took a minute to think about what Ktru had said before she said or asked anything else. Mya turned around in her seat, stared out the window, and then asked Ktru if she wanted her to drive. Ktru said yes. Mya and Ktru got out of the car and switched places. The girls got back in, put their seat belts on, and headed to school.

Halfway to school, Mya asked Ktru what had happened to Rainah. Ktru told Mya that after they left the party last night and Rainah dropped the Warriors off at home, Ktru received a call from Rainah's little sister. Rainah's sister told her that Rainah had fainted, and she was rushed to the emergency room. Ktru also told Mya that she called Rainah's little sister this morning to get an update on how Rainah was doing, and Rainah's sister said that she was in chemo.

Teardrops fell from Ktru and Mya's eyes. The Warriors knew about what happens at the end of leukemia, but none of them talked about it. They both knew that the situation was too sensitive to keep talking about, so Mya changed the subject and asked where Asia and Skyler were.

"Have you heard from Asia and Skyler?" Mya asked Ktru. "Naw," Ktru answered.

"I tried calling them this morning when I Facetimed you, but neither of them answered.

Mya sat and thought for a moment, and then she said, "Hopefully, we will see them when we get to school. Matta fact, try callin' em again." Ktru took out her phone and FaceTimed Asia and Skyler. Surprisingly, they both answered.

"OMG bitches! Why y'all didn't answer the phone when I called y'all earlier?" Ktru snapped. Asia replied,

"I don't know why Skyler didn't answer, but I was in the shower." Skyler then said, "Bitch I was gettin' some rise and shine dick." The Warriors all burst into laughter.

Skyler then said, "Is Rainah wit y'all because we tried calling her this morning and she didn't answer?" The looks on Mya and Ktru's faces let the others know that something was wrong.

"What bitches?" Asia snapped. Mya looked over at Ktru, and then Skyler yelled, "Somebody betta tell us the fuck something!" Ktru looked into the phone and softly said, "Rainah's little sister called me last nite, a lil after Rainah dropped us off, and she told me that Rainah fainted. She was rushed to the ER, and she has been in there since last night. Her sister also told me that Rainah was in chemo when she called me earlier this morning."

Skyler and Asia started balling. Their cries were so deep that Ktru and Mya started to cry as well. The Warriors all cried for like one minute and then Asia softly asked Ktru,

"Is she allowed to have any visitors?" Ktru answered, "Because of COVID, her sister told me that the only people that are allowed to see her are immediate family."

"Man fuck that shit. That's our muthafuckin' sister. I don't know how much more immediate you can git then dat!" Skyler snapped.

"I know that's the fuck right!" Mya added. The Warriors all sat silently for a few seconds, and then Mya said,

"Alright bitches. Are we sitting in our usual spot in the auditorium during the pep rally today?

"You already," Sklyer answered. "Alright. Say less. Ktru said.

"See you hoes 2nd period." The Warriors disconnected the call, and Mya and Ktru drove to The High in silence. As they drove up to the school, Juelz and Jihad were standing outside and Juelz's car looked like a thurst trap . Mya sucked her teeth and said,

"I swear to God. 'Des bitches is pressed." Ktru looked over at Jihad and said,

"I ain't stuntin' dat shit. Dat nigga know what time it is."

Mya parked the car three parking spots from Juelz. Her and Ktru jumped out of the car, walked past Juelz and Jihad without making any eye contact, and headed into the school. They were halfway up the steps and Jihad and Juelz came running up behind them.

"Aye, yo! Jihad yelled to Ktru.

"What fuck type time you on?" Ktru started smiling at Mya, and before she turned around, she gave Jihad a serious face.

"Nigga you was all caught up smiling and gigglin' in dem random bitches face. What you sweatin' me about?" Ktru asked. Jihad didn't respond. He just wrapped his arm around her neck, and they walked into the school.

Mya was headed to her homeroom, and Juelz came behind her, grabbed her by her waist, and pressed his dick up against her ass. Mya bent over like she was shocked to feel him behind her. Juelz spun Mya around, wrapped his hands around her waist, then cupped her big ass and he kissed her. Mya immediately became wet.

"Lemme see it" Juelz said to Mya. Mya pulled off her hoodie so that he could see her jersey.

"Umm. Dat looks good on you. Turn around lemme see it from the back," Juelz said. Mya smiled as she shyly turned around.

"Damn! Juelz said. Make sure you are in y'all spot second period."

"Ok," Mya answered. Juelz kissed Mya on the lips and then walked to the other side of the school.

Mya didn't feel much schooling today, so she decided to go down to their spot, which was in the basement. Mya wasn't sure if Mr. Junie was down there, but the way that she was feeling, she didn't care. As she headed down the stairs, she could smell that someone was down there blowin'.

'Damn. Mr. Junie, don't play no games," Mya laughed to herself. When Mya got to the bottom of the stairs, she was shocked as hell to see that it was Sam who was smoking. "What the fuck! Mya yelled.

"Yo. What the fuck is your deal bro?" Sam smiled as she blew smoke Mya's way.

"What? You think y'all the only muthafucka's that Mr. Junie is cool wit? Dat nigga fuck wit anybody that will get him high for free," Sam said.

"Whateva bitch. Where is Mr. Junie anyway? Mya asked. I need to talk to him." Sam didn't answer. She just pulled the wood as she looked at Mya.

"How the fuck I'm 'posed to know where dat nigga at? Do I look like his fuckin' keeper?" Sam answered. What Mya didn't know was that Mr. Junie's stabbed-up, dead body was stuffed in the back janitor's closet. Something didn't feel right to Mya, so she said. "Bitch. You know something." Sam took the last pull of the wood, tilted her head back and blew the smoke out in the air, stomped on the roach to put it out, then silently walked up the stairs.

CHAPTER 32

Mya walked around the basement, calling out to Mr. Junie. 'Mr. Junie? You down here? It's Mya," she yelled. There was nothing but silence. Mya looked behind the water heaters, and all, but no sign of Mr. Junie. Mya was walking towards the closet where Mr. Junie's body was and before right before she got to the closet, she received a FaceTime call from Rainah. Mya immediately forgot about finding Mr. Junie and channeled her excitement to Rainah.

"Heyyyyyyy boo!! We miss you!" Mya excitedly yelled. Rainah could be seen trying to force a smile and then Mya said,

"I'm so sorry sis. I don't wanna put no more stress on you." Rainah weakly replied, "Bitch stop trippin." They both started laughing. Mya was so glad to hear from her friend that she didn't know where to start.

Mya turned around and walked up the stairs to go to the auditorium to meet the rest of the Warriors. Rainah could see where Mya was, and as she walked up the stairs, Rainah asked,

"Where are the others? Why were you down at our spot alone?" The last thing Mya wanted to do was add more stress to Rainah, so she told her that she chose to skip first period down there.

"I'm on my way to the auditorium to meet the others and I want to surprise them," Mya said to Rainah.

Mya headed into the auditorium and looked for the Warriors and spotted them over in the corner.

"Hold on, sis. I am going to put the phone down and head over to them." Mya pushed her way through the rowdy crowd and when she finally reached the others Mya screamed, "Guess what bitches?!"

"Why you tweakin' bitch?" Skyler asked.

Mya took out her phone and flashed it in their faces. The Warriors all yelled louder than the big ass auditorium crowd. Ktru and Asia started crying and Skyler was waving her tears away, all dramatic style. Rainah looked at them and jokingly said,

"well say SOMETHING bitches!" They all started laughing. Asia then said, as she was wiping her eyes,

"All we wanna know is, are you ok? "Real shit." Ktru added. Rainah took a deep breath and lied as she said,

"Yess bitches. Who are we?" They all yelled out together, "The Muthafuckin' Warriors".

The girls started to laugh and then Rainah started coughing up spit.

"Well bitches. I have to go now. These freaky ass nurses are here to take me down for another round of chemo," Rainah said.

The Warriors laughed even though all they wanted to do was cry.

"You bitches go enjoy the pep rally and don't y'all be lettin' this shit ruin y'all day." Mya was about to say something, but the nurse got on the FaceTime call and said, "I'm sorry, but she has to go now. Either her or the family will be in touch to keep you updated," and then the nurse hung up the call. The Warriors all wanted to stay in their feelings, however as soon as the call hung up, the High band came doing their thang down the auditorium aisle and the energy of the place got rowdy.

"Come on bitches. You heard what our girl said. Let's do the dam thing!" Skyler yelled. The Warriors wasted no time being a part of the good vibes. They were all in the moment and then Mya received a text message from an unknown number. Mya opened up the text message and there was a picture of Mr. Junie's stabbed up, dead body in what she knew was the High's basement closet. Mya dropped her phone in shock and Asia quickly picked it up.

"Oh, my fuckin' God!" Asia yelled. Ktru and Skyler both went to grab the phone out of Asia's hand and when they did, Ktru took off to the school basement.

There was no need for any of the Warriors to try and question Ktru or try to change her mind, because it was mad loud in there and they knew she wouldn't hear them. The Warriors took off running behind Ktru and as Mya was runnin', she had the thought to call Juelz, but she forgot that he was a part of the pep rally. Ktru burst through the auditorium doors, ran full speed down the hall and darted down the basement stairs. The Warriors all headed to the closet where they had saw Mr. Junie's body, flung open the door and there was not anything in there, but cleaning supplies, a mop bucket and a broom.

"Don't nobody got time for this fuckin' shit! Asia screamed. Our friend is layin in her fuckin' death bed, muthafucka's gettin' shot, niggas trynna run us off the road, niggas shooting at our niggas. I just want this shit to stop!" Asia fell to her knees, and she loudly cried in her hands. Asia was the strongest one of the Warriors, so for them to see her like that, it hit different. It started to make the Warriors feel like they were defeated. Mya looked around at the rest of her crew and something that can't be explained, happened to her.

"I know what to do, Mya said. I need to use someone's car".

Mya thought that she was going to get a whole bunch of rah rah, however Ktru gave Mya her keys. Ktru said to Mya as she handed her the keys,

"I trust you. I just want you to let us know what you are going to do." Mya grabbed the keys from Ktru and said,

"I know where to get the answers that we are looking for. I need to go to our Secret Path." No one put up a fight, so Mya headed up the stairs, out of the basement and to the student parking lot. As Mya made her way to the car, she had no clue as to why she was being led to go the the Secret Path.

'Whatever the reason, I trust that is where I am supposed to be', Mya said to herself. Mya flung the car door open, hopped in, turned the ignition and mashed the gas. Mya skeeted out of the school parking lot like she was in the Fast and Furious.

'Damn bitch! Slow down. You gotta make it there in one piece,' Mya said to herself. Thoughts were running a thousand miles a minute through her mind as she tried to make sure she paid attention to traffic.

So much shit was going on inside Mya's head and then suddenly, a car struck her from the side, as she crossed the State Street bridge. The blow of the hit, smoove knocked Mya back into reality. 'What the fuck!' Mya yelled out to herself as she looked out of all of the mirrors to see what was going on. Mya looked through the passenger front mirror and lo and behold, there was the black boxed Chevy. 'You have got to be fuckin' kidding me!' Mya yelled out as she drove towards safety.

Mya and the black chevy were swerving from the left to right, while striking each other. Suddenly, the black chevy slammed on their breaks and Mya thought that the chicken fight was over. Out of nowhere, the Chevy slammed into the back of Mya's car, the car spun out of control, while Mya's body jerked onto the steering wheel. The Chevy stopped and came in one more time for the kill. This time, the hit was so powerful, that Mya's car flipped over the bank. Mya's car flipped three times as it rolled down the hill and crashed into a big oak tree.

CHAPTER 33

Mya's banged up, limp body laid in the wrecked car at the end of the bank, as she slowly came to. Panic began to set in because Mya not only didn't remember what had just happened, but she didn't know where she was. Mya started looking around and started scoping out the scenery, trying to figure out what was going on, then she heard the bushes shakin'. Mya heard footsteps and then a loud bang. The driver's side window had been busted out and she felt shattered glass fall on her. Mya stiffly turned her head to the left to see who this was.

Mya turned her head, vision blurry as hell, however she saw a dark shadow and suddenly, "BOOM". Mya felt a hard ass thump on the top of her head, causing her to be put to sleep. Mya was later awakened by some cold water that had been angrily splashed on her face. When Mya opened up her eyes, she could feel that her body stewas strapped in a seated position, on a chair. Mya raised her head and was ten inches facing away from Juelz. Mya began kicking and trying to wiggle her way out of the chair.

"Show your face. You fucking coward!" Mya screamed at the top of her lungs.

Mya had no clue where she was because it was mad dark, but she heard her voice echo when she yelled, so she knew that she was in a big, vacant building. Mya sat there screaming, kicking and trying to wiggle her way out of the chair, when the building lights suddenly lit up the place. Mya looked around and she could see that Skyler and Steph were strapped, back-to-back in chairs. Ktru and Jihad were strapped back-to-back, and Asia and Yao were strapped back-to-back, and they were all sleep. The kidnapper had on the same mask with the X for eyes, that was worn when she showed up alone at the warehouse.

It was at that point that Mya figured out they were in the same Warehouse that she met the masked person at, and this was more than likely the driver of the black boxed Chevy. The kidnapper walked around and began to angrily splash cold water on the rest of the gang. They all woke up with the same response as Mya. Juelz yelled out,

"Yo! What the fuck is going on?" "Oooooo my God. We are all going to die!" Skyler screamed.

"Shut the fuck up bitch! You don't even know what the fuck is going on!" snapped Ktru. Everyone started to panicking yelling and screaming. The kidnapper fired a warning shot in the air. The warehouse immediately got quiet.

"Now that's enough of that shit, muthafucka's! the kidnapper snapped. We have to set some ground rules so that I can keep some order around this bitch. This my shit and you niggas will only speak when spoken to, or else. Well, you'll just have to fuck around and find out." The kidnapper yelled. Now you might be asking yourself, why am I here? What is going on? Am I going to die? Who is this behind the mask? Blah, blah, blah, blah. The more you shut the fuck up, listen and don't ask me no fuckin' question, the faster all things will be known. Now if I have to keep talking to you, if you start poppin' fly, or try to escape, I will kill you without heazy. Now ladies and gentlemen without further ado, allow me to introduce myself."

The kidnapper slowly began to remove his mask. The gang looked at the kidnapper thinking about who the fuck this could be. The mask made it halfway off of the kidnapper's face when the masked person suddenly stopped and said, "You know what? How bout we start off with someone else?" The gang all looked around at one another.

"Patna' number one, come on down!" the kidnapper yelled out like he was the host of The Price is Right. From the right, out of the dark shadows, walked out bitch ass Dylan, with a smirk on his face.

"What the fuck?" Mya yelled out as she again tried to angrily wiggle her way out of the chair.

"Who the fuck is this nigga?" Yao asked. The kidnapper then said,

"My man. I don't think you are the nigga that should be asking me that question." The kidnapper walked over and stood a few inches away from Juelz and said, "I think this is where you should be asking who this nigga is." Juelz sucked his teeth and then spit on the kidnapper and said, "fuck you and that nigga!" The kidnapper pistol whipped Juelz and Mya and the gang started snappin' out. Threats, curse words and all types of shit was coming from the warriors and the brothers. That is until the kidnapper put the gun to Mya's temple and yelled out,

"Y'all are some hardheaded ass muthafucka's. Keep testing my gangsta and this bitch gone git a hot one right in her dome."

They quickly got quiet. "Now. Where were we? The kidnapper asked.

Oh yeah. My man Juelz. Don't you want to know who this is?" Juelz still didn't answer. The kidnapper became very annoyed and put the gun back on Mya's temple. "Alright man damn! Juelz yelled. Who the fuck is this clown ass nigga?"

"Well. I'm glad you asked" the kidnapper teasingly replied. Dylan why don't you tell this nigga who the fuck you are. Matta fact. Why don't you say it loud enough so that the whole gang can hear you loud and clear. Dylan stepped forward, stooped down and got a few inches away from Juelz's face and said,

"I am the nigga to whom yo' bitch LOVES givin' sloppy toppy!"

Juelz tried to jump forward out of his seat at Dylan. The kidnapper added injury to insult and said,

"In case you all didn't hear. This is the nigga who Mya's been faithfully swallowing up for the past year." Mya started yelling,

"Shut the fuck up!" Mya then looked at Juelz who had put his head down in disappointment. Mya looked at Juelz and began to plead by saying, "baby look at me! Please big dad, look at me! I am so sorry. I promise you I can explain!" Juelz didn't react. The kidnapper then started mocking Mya,

"Please baby look at me. I promise I can explain! Explain what bitch?

Why you're a fuckin' whore!" "Shut the fuck up! Mya yelled to the top of her lungs. You sit here and judge me, and you don't even know me. You fuckin' coward. Scared to show your mook ass face!"

The kidnapper angrily ripped the mask off his face. Mya thought she had seen a ghost. It was none other than the brother that Mya's mom gave to the father, Mitchell.

"Yea. see that gut punching feeling right there that you just felt? Mitchell asked Mya. That is the same feeling I felt when I found out that my fuckin' mother didn't fuckin' WANT ME! but yet still chose to have another family" Mitchell screamed in Mya's face. Mya started crying and said,

"Mitchell. I am so sorry that happened to you. I promise you. I just found out about you a couple of days ago. I can't imagine how you must be feeling, but you have to know that you are still my brother regardless of what happened."

"WRONG! Mitchell yelled out. I am not your brother. I am only of your DNA. You and none of those other bastards, are family to me! I hope you all rot in hell!"

Mitchell started scratching the side of his head with the tip of his pistol, while also pounding the other side of his head, with an open hand.

"I am tired of muthafucka's trynna mind fuck me. Matta fact. I have another muthafuckin' surprise for you SISSY!" Mitchell yelled. The gang sat in shock and awe as they waited for more drama to unfold. Mitchell looked at Mya and asked,

"You ready?" Mya did not respond. She sat in her chair, body slumped, head dropped while crying her eyes out. Mitchell started pacing back and forth and then he said to Mya, "SISSY, aren't you the least bit curious as to how Dylan and I met?"

Mya was silent and Mitchell continued to talk.

"Well, SISSY, imagine my surprise when I found out that Dylan killed our brother Mykel." Mya instantly sat upright in her chair, her jaw dropped, and she loudly screamed out in pain. All of a sudden, the rest of the Warriors started crying. Mitchell became annoyed by the crying and yelled out,

"All right! A fuckin' nuff. Listen the fuck up." Jihad looked at Mitchell and said, "Nigga, you betta kill me, because if you don't, you best believe I'ma put two hot one's in your fuckin' head!" Mitchell went over to Jihad and hit him on the top of his head with the butt of the pistol.

Ktru tried to jump out her chair, in an attempt to lunge at Mitchell and that's when Mitchell slapped her across the face. The Brothers and the Warriors were all hyped up. Dylan fired a warning shot in the air. Mitchell turned around and smartly said,

"Thank you patna." Dylan and Mitchell chuckled. Mitchell began to walk in a circle around everyone as he kept telling the story.

"Now. Where were we? Mitchell asked. Oh yea. So, imagine me finding out that this nigga Dylan had murdered my long-lost brother. How I found out about all of y'all is another story, but anyway. I find's this nigga, got em' to his knees, and was about to put one right between his eyes when he screams out,

"I know your sister Mya and she is worth 1 million dollars".

The gang was shocked as Mya sat in the chair feeling embarrassed.

"Oooooo. From the looks on everyone's face, y'all didn't know that our late great grandmother left Mya a million-dollar life insurance policy, which she can collect on her eighteenth birthday?" Mitchell said. Juelz looked Mya in her face and just shook his head in disappointment. Mya still didn't react. Mitchell looked at Mya and jokingly asked,

"Anything you wanna say SISSY?" Mya still didn't respond. Mitchell continued with the story.

"So, needless to say, I spared the nigga's life. You may all be asking yourself, well if he kills Mya, how does he eat from the million dollars? Excellent question people! Ding, ding, ding, ding. Guess who the money goes to if Mya dies. Yes! If you guessed our mother, then you guessed correctly. And guess who is gone to git in the good graces of our Mommie dearest by taking her on a major guilt trip? You guessed correctly again. ME!"

Mitchell continued to walk around as everyone sat in silence. "But wait there's more!" Mitchell yelled out. Mitchell looked at Juelz and mockingly said,

"Big dad. Here's another one just for you. Patna number two, COME ON DOWN!"

The gang looked around in every direction, anxious to see who was about to appear from outta the dark shadows. Sam came out from the back of the warehouse doing the Dougie. Mya dropped her head with even more shame. Mya slowly lifted her head and Juelz was staring her dead in the face, as if he already knew that Sam was another one of Mya's secret lovers.

Mya mouthed to Juelz, 'I'm sorry.'

Sam went directly to Mya and tried to tongue kiss her. Mya spit in Sam's face and then Sam smacked the shit out of her. Sam stood up, wiped the spit from her face and matter-of-factly said to Mya,

"Oh, you really think it's all about you, huh?" Sam walked away from Mya and headed over towards Ktru. Sam bent over and tried to tongue kiss Ktru and Ktru also spit in Sam's face. Sam then smacked the fire out of Ktru. Sam started laughing as Ktru yelled out to Mya,

"I swear to God Sis. I had no idea that you two were messin' around." Mya looked at Sam and coldly said to Ktru,

"Sis please. I ain't ever stunted' dis bitch!"

Jihad snapped the fuck out and said to Ktru,

"Why the fuck you apologizing to Mya, bitch? When the fuck you start scissoring bitches?" Ktru dropped her head in shame and Sam started talking.

"Oh. I see you muthafucka's got a lot of secrets in your so-called unbreakable gang. Well, allow me to add this Za to your wood. Juelz? Jihad?

Did you know that your bitches have been doing what you say, "scissoring" each other?" the kidnapper said.

"What the fuck?" Juelz and Jihad yelled out at the same time.

"You fuckin' cunt!" Mya yelled to Sam as she kicked her legs in anger. Sam mockingly rubbed her hands together as she smirked at the gang. "That's some shit for yo ass, right? Sam asked everyone.

Her pussy taste good as fuck don't it Ktru?" Juelz angrily started wiggling his body trying to get out of the ropes.

Sam looked at Jihad and said,

"Calm down killah" and then tapped him on the top of the head like she was petting a dog. Mitchell jumped up and down in the air and said,

 "This is some exciting shit ain't it? Betta then must-see TV." Mitchell started walking around, while tapping the pistol into his right hand. By this time, you must all think that you are in this shit because of my dear ole SISSY, huh? Well, That's false news. You sucka ass niggas are in this because of that hoe shit you pulled at The Square." Jihad, Yao, Juelz, Steph and Rock, all responded with different responses, and it became loud again. Sam fired a warning shot into the air. "Man fuck that shit bitch. Kill me!" Rock said as he spit at Sam. "O trust and believe it is gonna be my pleasure." Sam replied.

Mitchell said, "I am tired of you nigga's interrupting my script. You know what? Patna number three, COME ON DOWN!" Again, the gang looked around with surprise wondering who the fuck was gonna appear out of the shadows this time. They looked over to the right and Chloe, from The Valley Chicks, came from out of the shadows like she was walking on a catwalk.

"That's why my girl fucked you up. Fuckin' op!" Skyler yelled to Chloe as she spit at her. Chloe slowly walked by Skyler and rubbed her skinny ass against Skyler's shoulder. Chloe then headed towards Sam and started tongue kissing her. Sam playfully smacked Chloe on her ass. Chloe then walked over to Juelz, leaned over and tried to tongue kiss him, but Juelz turned his head from side to side, avoiding her kiss.

Mya really started kicking her legs and angrily wiggling her body trying to get out of the chair to get her hands on Chloe. Mitchell then said,

"What's the matter SISSY? You didn't know that your big dad was smashing Chloe?" Juelz looked Mya in the eyes and was about to say sorry and Mitchell interrupted and said,

"Nigga! After all these people that she is fuckin', you gone sit up here and apologize to her for fuckin' someone else? Damn SISSY! You must got some platinum plus, grade A pussy!" Mitchell started laughing loudly like he was a villian in a superhero movie. Mitchell then looked at Chloe and said to her,

"Why don't you do the honors?"

Chloe began to walk around and then said,

"Well bitches. Remember the day at the bowling alley when your rabid ass dog decided to charge at me like she was Bruce Lee and you bloodhounds jumped on my girls? Well, let's just say that my Brothers and his friends were the ones in the U Haul that tried to take you all out." Dylan then walked over and sexually kissed Chloe while grabbing her ass. Mitchell then said,

"Whew! I'm tellin' you man. I'm takin' this shit all the way to the top. Hollywood, here I come!" Mya looked at Mitchell with tears still running down her face and softly asked, "Who killed Mr. Junie?" Mitchell spun around and Sam said, "that would be me."

"Why? He has absolutely nothing to do with any of this," Mya snapped.

"O, I beg to differ SISSY. Somehow, and I still don't know how, that old ass nigga found out who are boss is. Sam went down to the basement to wait on ya dumb ass, SISSY, and she overheard Mr. Junie talking to himself. His crazy ass was saying out loud that the next time he sees y'all he was going to tell y'all who was trying to kill y'all and why. Now we couldn't have that could we? That old ass nigga tryna get in the way of me gettin' to a bag. Negative.

So just like that, that nigga had to go!" Mitchell yelled.

"Let us go, and we'll show you who the sucka ass niggas are!" Steph yelled out. Mitchell laughed at Steph and then looked at Mya and said,

"Anyway, as you can see, SISSY, we are all gonna live off of your death."

"Ova, my dead body!" Juelz yelled out.

Mitchell looked at Juelz and said,

"Yes, sir. That's the plan." Dylan, Sam, and Chloe started laughing.

Mitchell put his hands up in the air as if he was directing a choir and signaled for them to stop laughing. Mitchell then said,

"Now people. I know that this has been one hell of a joyride and now, it is time for the grand finale!" Everyone braced themselves for their end. Suddenly Mitchell started laughing all crazy style.

"Lighten up guys. I wasn't talking about the upper room finale. Not just yet. I was talking about everyone meeting the mastermind behind this beautiful master plan. And now without further ado, allow me to introduce..."

Again, everyone started looking for the person behind all of this to appear. Instead of a person appearing, out of nowhere, an armored truck crashed through the warehouse windows. Dylan, Mitchell, and Sam started shooting at the truck. The Warriors and the Brothers used all of their strength to fall down to the ground while tied to the chair. The charging truck was stopped by a large pole that was in the middle of the warehouse. Dylan, Mitchell, and Sam were still firing at the truck. Shots were then returned from the armored truck. Someone wearing a face mask came from underneath the truck and shot and killed Sam, Dylan, and Mitchell. On some John Wick shit. Somehow, Mya was able to free herself from the ropes. Chloe tried to run out of the warehouse and Mya tackled her to the ground.

Mya climbed on top of Chloe and angrily started banging her head against the concrete. Out of nowhere, Mya felt someone gently pulling her off of Chloe. Mya's body was numb from all the adrenaline. The masked hero hugged Mya. Mya's emotions were all over the place, so she felt like she had no choice but to hug this person back. Mya heard Juelz yell out,

"Hello. Can someone please untie us?"

Mya's body jerked back into reality, and she quickly ran over to Juelz and started untying him. The masked hero went around and randomly started untying everyone.

After everyone was untied, they all started hugging and kissing one another. Mya then asked the masked hero,

"Who are you?" The person slowly removed their mask. Mya dropped to her knees in shock. It was the brother who had disappeared without a trace two years ago. It was Mychael.

Mychael also dropped to his knees and hugged Mya. They tightly held each other, and Mya rocked him back and forth and cried uncontrollably.

Asia, Ktru, and Skyler all ran over and joined in on the family reunion hug. Rock came over to them and said to Mychael,

"That was a fuckin' good ass look, my nigga!" Mychael stood up and they dapped one another up. Yao, Juelz, Steph, and Jihad all followed suit.

Mya looked around for Chloe and said,

"Fuck! That bitch got away!" Mya looked at.

Mychael and said,

"That bitch knows who is behind all this bullshit." Mychael gently grabbed Mya by her face and softly said, "My Angel, I will make it my mission to find out who that person is, and I promise you this: I will bring you their head in a box as a gift."

TO BE CONTINUED

STILL RIDIN': REVENGE

COMING SOON